"I'll Be Forever Grateful To The School Principal Who Gave Me Your Name," Will Told Her.

He stood close, his hands on her arms. At the moment she was no longer thinking of him as Caroline's uncle, with a problem that needed her help. Instead, she could only see the handsome, sexy man who was inches away. She wanted to wrap her arms around him to kiss him. Her desire shocked her.

"I think you're bringing me back into the world and I'm not certain I'm ready," she whispered.

"You're ready," he said in a husky voice.

The moment she felt his lips, she closed her eyes. Her heart thudded. She had not been kissed by a man in six long years. His mouth settled possessively on hers, hard, demanding, no longer light and tentative.

"Will," she said, trying to get some firmness into her breathless voice. "You need to go."

Desire blazed in his dark eyes, making her racing heart pound faster. He wrapped his fingers in her hair. He wasn't going anywhere.

Dear Reader,

This story focuses on families—a theme that runs through many of my books because families are fascinating to me. Families are wonderful, unique, diverse, sometimes dysfunctional, but always interesting. *Relentless Pursuit* deals with different facets of love—that of an uncle devoted to his preschool niece whose scarred psyche developed after losing her single parent. The story also celebrates the love of a man and woman meeting, their excitement when falling in love and then their coping with seemingly insurmountable obstacles. Handsome Texas billionaire Will Delaney is too accustomed to getting his way to give up on what he wants.

Even though sandy-haired Ava Barton finds Will irresistible, she struggles to keep her distance because Will can derail all her dreams and well-laid plans for her future. For the first time in his life, Will has met his match in the beautiful educator. Also, the patriarch of the Delaney family, Argus Delaney, has recently passed away and the reading of his will brings new shocks to the Delaney family and changes lives with the legacies he bequeathed.

The story is set against a favorite backdrop—Texas. Larger-than-life in many aspects, the Texas romance plays out in Dallas and Austin settings.

The endless aspects in a relationship, its give-and-take as two people come to the realization they have found true love and struggle to overcome obstacles to a blossoming love, is what this story celebrates.

Thank you for selecting this book.

With best wishes,

Sara Orwig

SARA ORWIG

RELENTLESS PURSUIT

Recycling programs
for this product may
not exist in your area.

ISBN-13: 978-0-373-73172-5

RELENTLESS PURSUIT

www.Harlequin.com

Printed in U.S.A.

Books by Sara Orwig

Harlequin Desire

**_Texas-Sized Temptation_ #2086	‡_Pregnant at the Wedding_ #1864
**_A Lone Star Love Affair_ #2098	‡_Seduced by the Enemy_ #1875
**_Wild Western Nights_ #2110	‡_Wed to the Texan_ #1887
§_Relentless Pursuit_ #2159	**_Dakota Daddy_ #1936
	**_Montana Mistress_ #1941
Silhouette Desire	**_Wyoming Wedding_ #1947
	Tempting the Texas Tycoon #1989
Falcon's Lair #938	_Marrying the Lone Star Maverick_ #1997
The Bride's Choice #1019	**_Texas Tycoon's Christmas_
A Baby for Mommy #1060	_Fiancée_ #2049
Babes in Arms #1094	
Her Torrid Temporary	††Stallion Pass
Marriage #1125	*Stallion Pass: Texas Knights
The Consummate Cowboy #1164	†The Wealthy Ransomes
The Cowboy's Seductive	‡Platinum Grooms
Proposal #1192	**Stetsons & CEOs
World's Most Eligible Texan #1346	§Lone Star Legacy
Cowboy's Secret Child #1368	
The Playboy Meets	Other titles by this author
His Match #1438	available in ebook format
Cowboy's Special Woman #1449	
††_Do You Take This Enemy?_ #1476	
††_The Rancher, the Baby & the Nanny_ #1486	
Entangled with a Texan #1547	
*_Shut Up and Kiss Me_ #1581	
*_Standing Outside the Fire_ #1594	
Estate Affair #1657	
†_Pregnant with the First Heir_ #1752	
†_Revenge of the Second Son_ #1757	
†_Scandals from the Third Bride_ #1762	
Seduced by the Wealthy Playboy #1813	

SARA ORWIG

lives in Oklahoma. She has a patient husband who will take her on research trips anywhere from big cities to old forts. She is an avid collector of Western history books. With a master's degree in English, Sara has written historical romance, mainstream fiction and contemporary romance. Books are beloved treasures that take Sara to magical worlds, and she loves both reading and writing them.

With thanks to Stacy Boyd and Maureen Walters.
With love to my family.

One

William Delaney gazed into thickly lashed big brown eyes. While he loved his five-year-old niece with all his heart, this was the first time in his life he had had a problem with a female. Ever. From his earliest memories until now they always had given him smiles and laughter. He loved females and they loved him. Caroline's solemn gaze broke his heart.

He knelt to be level with the girl. Would he ever get accustomed to taking care of her? The responsibility weighed heavily and he was at a total loss—another first in his life.

"Here is a little present for you, Caroline. Just because you're a sweet girl." William watched her tiny hands tug free pink silk ribbon and silver paper to reveal a book.

She hugged the book, focusing on him. "Thank you," she whispered.

His heart skipped a beat with her simple thanks because he didn't always get that much response from her. "If you like it, I'll read it to you tonight. For now, after you have lunch, Miss Rosalyn will read your new book to you."

Caroline opened the book.

"I've got to go," William said, lightly embracing his niece thinking as he always did how frail she seemed. "As soon as I get home tonight, I'll come see you," he added, releasing her. His heart thumped when big brown eyes stared at him. "Miss Rosalyn has your breakfast ready."

The nanny smiled at the girl and took her hand. "We have oatmeal plus one of your favorites—strawberries," she said brightly.

As Will left, he hoped Caroline would eat something. Too many times in the year since he'd become her guardian, she would take only a few bites and then sit politely while he finished.

He drove his black sports car through the gated area in Dallas where he lived and headed for his private jet.

At half past eleven, he walked through the doors of an Austin restaurant where he was meeting a teacher. She had been recommended as a superb educator and one who could suggest excellent tutors for Caroline.

One more effort to find help for his niece. Since his brother's death in a plane crash the previous summer, Will had spent the past school year talking to Caroline's pre-kindergarten teacher, her tutors, her counselors, the child psychiatrists and the pediatricians. None had helped bring Caroline out of the shell she had retreated into with the loss of her parent. The death of her dad, plus her mother walking out of the marriage when Caroline was a baby, had been too much.

Will had never met Ava Barton. All he knew, aside from her great reputation, was that she was widowed. He had formed an image in his mind of someone who resembled one of his own elementary school teachers. When he entered the waiting area, he expected to see spectacles, graying hair and a smiling face.

The lobby was already becoming crowded. As he looked

around, his attention was caught by a gorgeous sandy-haired blonde who met his gaze. Distracted, he momentarily forgot the teacher while he glanced swiftly from straight, silky hair that cascaded below her shoulders down to a tiny waist. Her short tan skirt revealed her knees, long legs and dainty feet in high heels.

His gaze traveled back to lock on her wide eyes, so green he could only stare and forget the purpose of his appointment.

Seemingly as captured in the moment as he was, she stared back at him. While seconds ticked past, her eyes widened a fraction. When she walked toward him, images of any teachers he had ever had vanished. The realization that he might actually be facing Ava Barton shook him. He should have a professional relationship with a teacher, but the relationship he wanted with the woman walking toward him was strictly that of a man attracted to a gorgeous woman. The tension that rocked him made him want to know her better, and his desire had nothing to do with her job.

He regained his wits. "Ava Barton?"

"Yes," she replied, offering her hand.

Her dazzling smile heated his insides. Her hand was warm, delicate, soft. He regretted having to let go the sizzling contact.

Fighting to keep his focus on her face and not yield to the temptation to look her over again from head to toe, he released her hand. "I'm William Delaney, Caroline's uncle and guardian," he explained. His secretary had arranged this appointment, and now he regretted not giving more time and attention to Ava Barton's background beyond teaching.

"I'll get the maître d'."

Within minutes they were seated in a quiet area near a splashing fountain.

"You're not what I expected," he admitted as soon as they were alone. She had a smattering of freckles across her nose, but otherwise her skin was smooth, pale with rosy cheeks.

Her lips were full, enticing and as he focused on her mouth, he wondered what it would be like to kiss her. Another unprofessional curiosity. He was going to have to make a choice in dealing with her: keep it strictly business, or do what he wanted and get to know her as a woman. When he looked into her big green eyes, the decision seemed clear to follow his heart. He shrugged away a swift surge of guilt because he usually could follow a professional course with ease. But when he looked at her, he knew there was no way he could stay businesslike.

"Teachers come in all sizes and shapes," she said. "You're what I expected, but then I've seen your pictures in the newspapers and Texas magazines."

"You don't look like any teachers I ever had. I might have been more enthused about school if I'd had you for a teacher."

"I doubt it," she said, giving him another dazzling smile.

"You have no idea. I could have been the studious type."

"You look like the sports—no, the debate type."

"You're an observant teacher. Or good at guessing."

Before she could answer, their waiter appeared, took their drink orders of two glasses of water and left them with menus.

"I appreciate you meeting with me," Will said. "You have an impressive resume and you've been highly recommended by Caroline's principal and her teacher. The teacher she'll have next year is using one of the textbooks you authored."

"Thank you. I feel strongly that nearly all children can be taught to read." She tilted her head to study him. "If we had talked on the phone, it would have saved you the trip to Austin. I already gave your secretary a list of qualified tutors, so I assume you want to discuss the candidates."

He nodded. "I wouldn't have missed this lunch for the world," he said, not just because Ava could help Caroline, but because he was enjoying her company himself, too. She was stunning, and it was difficult to keep his mind on his mission.

"Your secretary told me about your niece, Caroline. She's had trauma in her young life."

"She lost her single-parent dad over a year ago, and after the accident she shut out the world."

"What about her mother?"

"She walked out when Caroline was four months old."

"Four months? What kind of marriage was that?"

"The kind the men in my family have had. Mom and Dad divorced and it was bitter. But we were all older than Caroline. I was fourteen. Marriage is not an institution that holds appeal for any of the males in my family."

She had a slight frown as she stared at him intently. "Two marriages gone sour doesn't mean all marriages are bad."

"We do well in the financial world. Not so great in personal lives. With her mom gone as far back as she can remember, Caroline poured all her love on her dad. When she lost him because of the plane crash, it was devastating to her."

"Does her mother ever see her?"

"She gave up all rights when she left."

"What kind of mother does that?" Ava asked, her green eyes open wide. Sea-green eyes he could gaze into all day.

"The kind of beautiful woman whose total focus is on herself, who loves money and things money can buy. When they dated, my brother was wild and a partying man. She liked to party. When they married, he settled like a rock, but she didn't want to give up the party life, or take responsibility even though in our family she would have had all the staff she wanted. They agreed to postpone a family until later, and then Caroline was a surprise that didn't go over well with her mother."

"Caroline is young for the kind of loss she's had. It hurts terribly and I'm sorry."

He glanced at the wedding ring on her finger. "I'm sorry for your loss. I see you're still wearing your ring."

Looking down, she touched her ring while her sandy hair swung forward on both sides of her face, making him want to run his fingers through the long strands.

"I wear my ring because I'm not interested in dating, and it keeps men from inviting me out. I loved my husband and losing him was dreadful. I don't ever want to run that risk again."

He studied her. "So you've given up on men, marriage and life in general."

"Not life in general. I love kids and working with them. You don't sound as if you have plans for marriage in your life."

"I definitely do not. I'm not getting into that trap. With the Delaney men's track record, marriage means heartbreak, bitterness and loss. No, thank you. How long have you been widowed?" he asked, expecting her to reply a year or less.

"Six years now. We were undergraduates in college when we married and he was killed in a motorcycle accident that first year of our marriage."

"Sorry."

"Thanks. You didn't come here to discuss my history. Tell me about Caroline."

"Caroline has withdrawn from the world. Maybe it's defensive—if she doesn't love, maybe she won't get so hurt with loss. I've heard all kinds of theories, but that one makes the most sense. Caroline talks very little. She is unresponsive to people, and consequently she has performed poorly in preschool. She keeps to herself and doesn't associate with other kids. It didn't help when my father died recently, because he doted on her since she was the only grandchild. Even so, they weren't really close. It was just one more thing that hurt her. She became a little more receptive with me after he was gone because I think she feels we both share a loss."

"I'm sure you've had all kinds of help for her."

"I've tried everything. That's why I'm here." He studied her in silence a moment. "You don't approve of me, do you?"

She blinked and then her eyes widened and she blushed, a rosy pink filling her cheeks. "I didn't know it showed."

A slight annoyance pricked him. He was unaccustomed to negative reactions from females.

"I'll admit, I may have jumped to inaccurate conclusions because of your press," she continued. "I'm glad you're concerned about Caroline. But have you tried giving a little more of yourself?" she asked quietly.

Startled, he stared at her. When annoyance flashed briefly, he tried to curb it. "I don't know anything about little girls. I've done everything I can think of to do."

"Do you spend a lot of time with her?"

With an uncomfortable guilt at not being able to reach his niece, he frowned. "I try. She doesn't respond to me as much as she used to when her dad was living. I have to admit that I don't give her the hours of attention her father did. For the first time in my life, I'm up against something I can't cope with."

"If you're trying, that's important."

"Caroline's doctor said if she responds to someone, we should maintain the relationship as much as possible. Unfortunately, so far, I haven't found a single person she reacts to with enthusiasm. She used to have a sunny disposition. Now, instead of a joyous little girl, she's quiet, polite and withdrawn. Her nanny and my staff all try to pamper her, but it doesn't seem to matter to her."

He picked up his menu. "We better decide on something to eat before we get too deep in this conversation. Our waiter will return soon. Do you see anything that appeals to you?"

She laughed lightly. "It all appeals to me. This is one of my favorite places to eat."

"It's one of mine, too" he said, staring in surprise. "When

I'm in Austin, I eat here. I can't recall seeing you. I'd remember."

As she shook her head, she smiled. "No, you wouldn't. We were strangers until today. Even though this is a favorite restaurant, I come at odd hours and not often." She closed her menu. "I do eat here often enough that I know what I want."

"It's always good when you know what you want," he said, watching Ava as the waiter returned and she ordered a Cobb salad and raspberry iced tea.

He ordered a hamburger, and as soon as they were alone, Will added, "On the flight here, I looked over the resumes of the teachers you recommended."

"I've given you highly qualified, experienced teachers who have very successful track records in raising children's reading levels."

"I know, and I appreciate that. But it's more difficult to choose a tutor than I realized. I'm worried about kindergarten because Caroline is going to have to participate and show her teacher what she can do. She'll be in a private school and they'll work with her, but there's just so much they can do. When she doesn't respond at all, people give up trying to help her as much."

"Hopefully the right tutor might make a difference."

"Right now, Caroline is the most important person in my life. Before we go further, I'd like to fly you to Dallas and have you meet Caroline. I think it would be better if you know her. Once you meet her and spend a little time with her, you might be able to better assess the situation. Since time is valuable, I'll make the trip worth your while. Two thousand a day plus expenses, and I'll fly you to Dallas and back to Austin."

"That's an enormous amount to pay," she said, not hiding her surprise.

"I can afford it, and this is top priority," he stated, determined to get what he wanted.

"You know there are excellent private schools where you can board her and they work with the children all day and have activities at night."

He could tell the question was a test, but one he knew he'd pass. "I'm not sending her away."

Her green eyes flashed. "That's commendable."

"Will you come to Dallas?"

While he waited for her answer, his pulse sped. He wanted her to accept his offer, and it wasn't altogether because of Caroline. This morning he had expected to fly to Austin, have lunch, go over the candidates and fly home, mission accomplished. Instead, from the first moment he looked at Ava, he had scrapped his original plan and purpose and was going by instinct, determined to get help for Caroline but also to get to know Ava.

"When are we talking about?" she asked.

"Whenever you want. You can fly back with me now. Fly tomorrow or next week. Whenever you can work the trip into your schedule, but the sooner, the better."

As she gazed beyond him while she thought it over, he took the opportunity to study her again. Her silky hair was meant for a man's hands to tangle. Thick, long sandy lashes framed her seductive eyes. The sight of her mouth made his temperature climb. All he wanted to do was flirt, ask her out, take her to dinner and then kiss her until they were both on fire. She didn't want to be entangled with anyone and he didn't, either, so passion would not lead to complications.

The waiter brought their orders. As soon as they were alone she leaned forward. "What time are you returning to Dallas?"

"I have one appointment at three this afternoon to stop by the office of one of my customers. It won't take long and then I planned to fly home. I can change my schedule easily."

"In a couple of hours I can be ready to return with you tonight if you'd like. The weekend is coming up, plus I have a few days with nothing scheduled."

"Excellent. We'll fly home and you can meet Caroline. Stay a week if you can."

She smiled. "It won't take that long to get to know Caroline a little. I'll stay tonight and tomorrow night and fly back Saturday. I just got my doctorate and I plan to spend the summer and this next year working on opening my own private school."

"That's admirable," he replied, his pulse humming because she would be at his house for the next three days and he could get to know her.

"I assume you read to Caroline," she said. "If you can give me a list of some of her favorite books, I might be able to add to them with a new book or two."

"Sure. Better yet, when we finish lunch, I'll take you to a bookstore and we can look things over and get what you want."

"As long as you still leave me a couple of hours to get ready to go."

He couldn't imagine what she would have to do that would take a couple of hours because she looked ready now except for packing clothes and necessities. "You take all the time you want."

"You're very determined about this."

"I'd do anything to help Caroline. I know what she was like before she lost her father."

"I think I've misjudged you. I had preconceptions built by tabloids and television," she admitted.

"It's good news to discover your opinion of me is improving. Hopefully, we'll get better acquainted."

She smiled. "I'm flying to Dallas to get to know Caroline."

"I'll have to work on my image. I'm not accustomed to having someone I'm with tell me she is not interested in getting to know me."

"It really isn't important that we become buddies," she said, pausing over her salad.

"It will be far more fun, and you might be surprised what you discover. I know I want to get to know you," he said, his voice lowering a notch.

"I ought to tell you no flirting," she said, shaking her head, "but I suspect that's impossible. I imagine at this point in your life, it's as much a habit as breathing."

"And where a beautiful woman is concerned—as necessary. You'll be gone in two days, so what does a little flirting hurt?"

"Maybe you deserved your media coverage after all."

"Forget the media. I really don't know that much about you except you're excellent in dealing with children and reading. You've taught and you said you recently earned a doctorate."

"Correct."

"What do you plan to do with the degree?"

"I publish texts on teaching reading, children's books on reading and games. Hopefully, the degree lends more credibility. I plan to open a private school—at this point, limited to first and second grade—and use some of my own methods for reading instruction. I'm working on securing grants. I have limited funds for this."

"Opening a school is ambitious," he said with admiration, reassessing his opinion of her. "A woman with drive." And one who hoped to get grants for the financial backing—a bargaining point that gave him an advantage.

Beautiful, driven and intelligent—an enticing combination that excited him.

"A lot of the praise I received about you was about your ability to work with children," he stated.

"I like kids and feel at ease with them. I have younger siblings. I try to make all this interesting and appealing to kids. Not necessarily easy, because learning isn't always easy. I love working with kids and want to dedicate my life to them."

"How many siblings?"

"I have two younger sisters, Trinity and Summer. Trinity is a technical writer for an exclusive Austin clothing store chain. My youngest sister is home for the summer. She'll be a sophomore in college and wants to teach."

"Parents? And where's home?"

"My dad has a feed store in Lubbock and my mom is a dental hygienist. So what about your family other than Caroline?"

"Besides my late brother, Adam, I have two other brothers. Zach, who is rarely home because of his job, and the youngest, Ryan, works in Houston. My parents divorced years ago, and my mother is twice remarried and lives in Atlanta now. My dad recently passed away and his estate isn't settled yet. That's it."

"Your brother who is rarely home—does he have any responsibility in Caroline's care?"

"No. I'm her guardian and I've always been closer to her and to Adam. He was born three years before I was. Zach is thirty-two, four years younger than I am. He's in demolition and travels because he works in Europe and Japan—all over the world, actually. He's good at what he does, but rarely home. Ryan is twenty-nine. He's the one who lives in Houston and has taken over a drilling company we own. None of us are really daddy material."

"So tell me about Caroline, as well as her nanny. What does she like to do? All kids have something they like."

"Swimming. If you like to swim, bring your swimsuit. It's a way to interact with her. Also, she likes to read."

"She's five and can read—that's early, and it's good news."

"She won't participate at school, so they don't know how well she reads. I tell her teacher that she reads at home, but since she won't read at school or say what she's read, her teacher is skeptical."

"Do you think Caroline is really reading?"

"I know she is. She started reading very simple books before her dad was killed. The beginner Dr. Seuss books, for example."

"She was young to be reading like that."

"Her dad doted on her and worked with her. She's a sharp kid, so that makes her withdrawal painful. If it was a book she liked, she would talk at length about what she read. I give her books because that's one thing that seems to please her."

"I take her reading as a hopeful sign. If she likes to read, it will give her tutor a chance to reach her."

He glanced at their plates. "We're both finished. Would you like dessert? They have great ones."

"No, thanks. We'll head for the bookstore. There's one close."

He escorted her to a waiting limo. At the bookstore Will held the door for her, watching the slight sway of her hips as she entered, momentarily forgetting his mission while he thought about Ava. He wanted to ask her out for an evening where no business would be discussed.

She led him to the children's section and began to pick out books. "How about this one?"

"Caroline has that book and likes it," he said, looking at a familiar story. "I can't remember everything she has. Get what you want and I'll call Rosalyn and ask her."

"I can bring it back if she already has it." While Ava strolled along the row of books, Will watched her, catching up with her when she stopped to pull out a book.

"That you have no men in your life surprises me. And six years is a long time."

"I'm not interested in going out with anyone. Actually, I'm too busy."

"No one is that busy."

She paused to smile at him. "And you're offering to fill the void? Let's stick to finding a tutor for your niece and then we'll go our separate ways. Unfortunately, I don't know many single, cute young tutors."

"Under different circumstances, I would agree with you about going our separate ways, but there's something going on here that prevents that," he said, lowering his voice and stepping closer to her. Her eyes widened a fraction as she gazed at him.

"The electricity. You feel it the same as I do. Deny that," he challenged softly, reminding himself in two days she'd be out of his life. This woman was too earnest for him. Ambitious, serious—not his type. But the next two days could be interesting.

She inhaled deeply and her cheeks flushed as she looked away. "Be that as it may, we're sticking to books and reading and business," she whispered. "There's no place in my life for a brief affair. If I ever get involved with another man, it will have to be a deeply committed relationship. I doubt if that's what you're looking for."

"Definitely not. I'm not into a strong commitment, a lasting relationship or marriage. No male in my family has done well in those situations."

"Then we shouldn't start even a casual relationship." She moved along the row of books. "Does she have this?" she asked, withdrawing a first reader with bears on the cover.

His hand closed over Ava's as she held the book. At the instant of contact she drew a deep breath, causing his pulse to speed a notch. She reacted to every personal remark or gesture, each touch.

"No. Not that I can recall," he replied, looking at the cover.

"It's a cute story. I'll get this one."

"You know your children's books."

"My doctorate is in early reading. I should know them."

"If you're getting more, I'll hold the books you want while you look." It occurred to him that she might be the perfect tutor for Caroline. A doctorate degree, dedicated to children—she was imminently qualified.

"Oh, yes," she answered, moving away from him. He watched her, something easy to do. She would be at his house for two days. He made a mental note to clear his calendar and stay home with her the entire time. He would get past the barriers she had thrown up. If she hadn't dated in six years, she was long overdue. He had not been fabricating the sizzling tension that existed since the first moment he saw her. She felt it as much as he did; she had not denied feeling it.

"What about this book?" she asked, holding out one with puppies on the cover.

He held one corner. "Let's see the pictures," he said, moving closer and catching the scent of her perfume. She turned the pages while he enjoyed standing close. As far as he knew, Caroline did not own the book, but he was savoring the moment. "I don't think she has this one."

"I love this story. Put this with the other one," she said, handing the book to him and continuing her search. After she selected four books, they had a brief argument about who would pay, which he won.

"When do you want me to come pick you up?" he asked as they headed out and toward her home.

"Early evening. I'll be ready," she said.

He nodded. "Good enough. I'll take the books because they're going home anyway."

"Fine. Thank you, and thanks for the lunch. I'll see you soon," she said at the door. He watched her step into the building before he returned to the limo.

She was flying home with him, and he would have the next couple of days to try to talk her into staying this summer and tutoring Caroline herself. He had already made a decision about who he wanted to tutor Caroline. None of the tutors on her list were as qualified or had the great references that Ava did. She was the best possible person, and he had long ago learned it was usually worth more to get the best. Whatever Ava decided, he intended to get to know her. The challenge she presented was irresistible when it involved a beautiful woman who had drive and intelligence.

Ava stood at the window and watched the limo disappear down the street. She wasn't ready for the complication of a man in her life, and William Delaney would be a big-time complication. Sparks had flown from the first moment they saw each other in the restaurant lobby—something that hadn't happened to her since Ethan. Something she hadn't wanted to have happen now. She could vividly recall the moment: taller than others in the lobby, Will had stood out from the crowd as he walked through the door. She had seen pictures of him in Texas magazines, the newspaper, local news, but they hadn't done him justice. He had to be six-four. His compelling chocolate eyes, fringed with thick, slightly curly lashes had taken her breath. His thick wavy black hair was as appealing as his other features and together—eyes, hair, firm jaw—all made a lethal combination that packaged seduction. A supremely confident man with good reason. Born into wealth, life had been on his terms—most of the time. She suspected the problems with his niece had really thrown him. Caroline was a lovable frustration he was totally unaccustomed to facing.

Ava pulled her list of tutors out of her purse. It started with the one she thought the most qualified and the best to work with a traumatized child. Becky Hofflinger was wonderful with children and a highly successful tutor. Becky could use the money, and Ava guessed Will would be extremely generous.

She thought about the two thousand she would get paid for each day in Dallas. She could have stayed a week and he would gladly have paid her. She shook her head. The man had more money than one human needed.

Fly to Dallas, meet his niece and assess the little girl. From the first moment her heart had gone out to the child. It was heart-wrenching to lose a loved one, and for a child to lose her only parent in a tragic accident had to be devastating. Ava empathized. Her heartbreak and grief had diminished somewhat, although there were moments it hit again.

She didn't want another relationship; she couldn't imagine having one. Her own reaction to Will had shocked her. For the past six years she had lived in memories and hurt, trying to overcome loss. No one had held the tiniest bit of interest for her. Until Will Delaney came into her life.

As she showered and then dressed in red slacks, a matching red silk blouse and high-heeled red sandals, she had to admit she admired Will's concern for his niece even more so because she had never expected that of him. She'd jumped to hasty conclusions.

Only time would tell.

Two

The buzzer rang, and Ava pressed the intercom listen button.

"Ava, I'll come get your things." Will's deep voice had a slightly husky note, definitely unique and unforgettable.

When she opened her door, the impact of seeing him again was as electric as it had been the first time. Maybe more, she decided, too aware her pulse raced. He was breathtaking, too handsome, and getting to know him had revealed a caring man, which was a devastating combination. Along with his navy suit jacket, he had shed his tie. With the top three buttons unfastened on his snowy dress shirt, he looked more casual. Warm approval in his brown eyes gave her a rush of pleasure.

"You look great," he said.

"Thank you. For our purposes though, it wouldn't matter if I wore a tent and sported floor-length hair."

"On you the long hair and tent would look good," he said, smiling at her. Her heart skipped at that irresistible smile. Trying to get her mind off him, she turned away to retrieve her small bag and a carry-on suitcase, which he picked up before she could.

Within an hour they were airborne. She looked below at Austin. Sunlight splashed on the red granite of the state capitol as the plane headed north.

"Does Caroline know we're coming now?" Ava asked, her pulse leaping when she turned to look into his brown eyes.

"Yes. She won't come running. You'll see how subdued she is. When her dad was alive, she wasn't reserved at all. They were really close and he loved her more than anything."

"That's sad that she doesn't have him now. Was she cooperative with him?"

"Yes. A bright, happy, cheerful little girl. That's what hurts so badly. She's drawn into a shell and no one has been able to reach her. It breaks my heart because I know what a sunny disposition she had."

Since he sounded truly hurt, she was touched again by his concern. If she were going to be with him longer than two days, she would need a more solid barrier around her heart. She looked out the window, trying to think of another subject.

"Do you travel a lot? Will you be around while I'm there?"

"Yes. I'm not going to drop you off and leave," he replied with a smile. "I'll take time off from work and be home as much as possible."

"After I meet Caroline, I'll need time alone with her, so you go ahead and work tomorrow."

"I'll give you time alone. I can stay out of the way. I hope you brought a swimsuit."

"I did," she said, feeling tingly at the thought of swimming with Will. "Does she have a schedule for her day?"

"Her schedule is flexible in the summer. Breakfast and then reading and playtime. Sometimes a swim before lunch if she wants to. Lunch, a quiet time of reading—I think she just reads because she doesn't nap any longer. Then, usually swims again. Our nanny, Rosalyn, is with her all day. I try to be home for dinner and spend the evening with her and put her to bed. If I need to work late or attend a social event, her nanny spends the evening playing with her. Caroline has every kind of toy imaginable and she's getting amazingly good with computers."

"I'm sure," Ava replied, smiling at him. "Her situation sounds challenging, but I have a short list of tutors who come highly recommended. After my assessment, I'll be able to choose the one who can hopefully work a miracle."

"I hope so. It's been a godsend to find you. Every day when I'm with Caroline, this situation tears me up. I owe it to my brother and I love Caroline. I'm praying she can be helped. I think the right person can reach her. I want to hire the best possible person to work with her."

"We'll see. These are the most qualified tutors I know. I asked each one if I could put her on my list, so I found out who was available and who wasn't. At present, all three women are employed, but their service will be ending very shortly and they'll be free to take on a new challenge."

"Good. I'll make it worthwhile for the person I decide will do the most for Caroline."

"I'm sure of that. What you're paying me is generous, to say the least."

"This is worth it."

She smiled at him. "You're a good uncle, Will Delaney."

He leaned closer.

"And you, Ava, have the greatest smile. I'll see if I can keep you smiling."

"That isn't one of the week's requirements. I'm here about Caroline. Only about Caroline," she said, her heart racing, something she couldn't control.

"Maybe I can change your mind on that, too."

"Too? What else?"

"Let's see how it goes with Caroline."

She wondered what he referred to. He surely didn't want to hire her, because she was not a tutor. When he sat back, her drumming pulse returned to normal.

The flight was quick and a limo was waiting.

As soon as they drove through the gates where he lived, her mounting curiosity about his niece momentarily abated, replaced by fascination with the mansion she glimpsed through the trees as they wound up the drive.

"You have a beautiful estate. This fits the image I had of you much more than the doting uncle you are."

"I need to change some of your preconceived notions about me. We'll get to know each other. I'm looking forward to it."

"That's not on this agenda. I'm here about Caroline and I think that's the second time already that I've reminded you."

"Relax and lighten up. We can get to know each other while you meet and learn about my niece. One doesn't rule out the other. They're both going to happen."

"You're not paying any attention to me," she said.

"Not true at all. I'm paying a great deal of attention to you and I'm slipping, if you haven't noticed."

"Will you stop flirting?" she asked, amused and unable to be really annoyed with him over harmless flirting, yet afraid of her volatile reaction to him intensifying.

"Not on this night. Why should I? Flirting is fun, harmless and I like the exchange when I'm with a gorgeous woman. You're not interested in anything serious and neither am I. We should make a good pair."

"Thank you for the compliment. And we're not going to be 'a pair.' I think this conversation needs to shift to another topic. Your palatial home is magnificent. You live here with just Caroline and her nanny?" Ava could clearly see the elegant mansion. Sunlight splashed over the gray slate roofs and gave a warm tint to the pale stones.

"We'll come back to the conversation we were having, but to answer your question—it's a comfortable house built to suit me. It's big enough for all of us and my staff. A partial staff is on the third floor." She turned to watch him, listening and thinking at the same time that she hadn't had a clear concept of his wealth.

"The head gardener and his staff have homes on my grounds. So does my cook. My chauffeur has a house near the garage."

She barely heard him as she stared at the sprawling three-story home built in the style of an English country manor surrounded by landscaped grounds and sprinklers watering beds of colorful flowers. More flowers surrounded a large circular three-tiered fountain with sparkling water tumbling over each tier.

"A little girl will be lost in this," Ava said without realizing she had spoken aloud.

"Caroline's accustomed to it. The house she lived in with her dad was very similar to mine. I doubt if she gives it a thought."

"All this wealth, yet you can't accomplish the one thing you want to do," she said quietly and he glanced her way.

"You're right. At least it gives me options on getting help for her. I can't stop thinking that if I keep trying, I'll find that perfect person who'll get her to open up."

"I hope you do," she said, touched again by his concern for his niece.

At the front they climbed out of the car to cross the wide porch. The massive door swung open and a butler greeted them. Ava entered a three-story-high walnut-paneled entryway where a huge French Empire chandelier hung overhead.

"Ava, meet Fred Simms. This is Ms. Barton, Fred."

"Miss Caroline is in the library with Miss Rosalyn," Fred said after greeting Ava.

Will held Ava's arm. "This way," he said. She was as aware of his fingers resting on her forearm as she was of his palatial mansion.

Ava carried two of the books, each in colorful sacks from the bookstore. They entered the library, where a child sat drawing at a table. Her nanny sat nearby, also drawing.

Pausing, Caroline turned to look at them, sliding out of her chair while the nanny came around the table.

"Look who's here, Caroline," the nanny said cheerfully.

Ava looked at a beautiful child with long curly black hair, thickly lashed big brown eyes and a facial structure bearing a clear family resemblance to her uncle. She was a feminine version of him.

Caroline gazed solemnly at Will in silence as he picked her up gently to kiss her cheek. "How's my girl?" he greeted her, smiling. "I want you to meet someone." He turned to face Ava.

"Caroline, this is my friend, Miss Ava. She's a teacher."

Caroline stared in silence at Ava.

"Ava meet Caroline."

"I've heard a lot about you, Caroline, and I'm so glad to meet you," Ava said.

"Ava, this is our nanny, Rosalyn Torrence. Rosalyn, meet Ava Barton."

"I'm glad to meet you," Ava said, shaking hands with the nanny. She turned her attention back to Caroline.

"I've missed you, sweetie," Will said in such gentle tones Ava's heart lurched. "I'm glad to be home. We'll stay with her now, Rosalyn."

"Thank you. If you want me, I'll be upstairs."

"Thanks," he replied. As Rosalyn quietly left, he set Caroline on her feet.

Ava held out two of the sacks. "Caroline, I brought you a present."

Caroline stared at the sacks, eyeing them and making no effort to take them.

"Look at the presents, sweetie," Will urged

Caroline obediently took the bags and pulled out the first

book, looking at it intently. "Thank you," she whispered so softly Ava barely heard her. She pulled out the second book.

"Thank you," she whispered again.

"You're welcome," Ava said, kneeling so she would be on the same level with Caroline. "I'll read them to you whenever you want to hear them."

Caroline nodded, looking at Will.

"You can whenever you want," he said. "I'll get out of the way. Want to read them now?"

Caroline shook her head no.

"I'll go unpack then," Ava said far more cheerfully than she felt. She was not a child psychiatrist, but it seemed to her that Will had just as big a problem as he had described. The child seemed remote, cold and unresponsive, as if she wanted to shut herself away from all human contact.

"I'll stay with Caroline, but first," he said, picking up Caroline again. "Let's go show Miss Ava where she will be sleeping."

Upstairs, they turned to the east wing and passed beautiful rooms until he led her into a suite. "How's this?" he asked. "You'll be near Caroline's room."

"This is gorgeous," Ava exclaimed, looking around a suite lavishly outfitted with an antique rose silk sofa, Louis XIV–style furniture and a thick rug on the polished oak floor. Through the open door she could see the bedroom. "I'll unpack, which won't take long. I can find my way back to the library."

"Leave your things to unpack later. C'mon. We'll give you a brief tour so you know where you are."

Noticing how silent Caroline was, docilely letting Will carry her without wiggling or the usual chatter of a child her age, Ava was more aware of the child than her surroundings.

"Here's Caroline's suite," he said, pausing at a doorway a brief distance down the hall. "Rosalyn is in an adjoining suite, although she has a bed in Caroline's room."

They entered a child's room that was a dream room to Ava. Murals of nursery characters decorated one wall. White clouds were painted on the pale blue ceiling. The furniture was painted white, or covered with pink and blue chintz upholstery. Table legs were carved as nursery characters. She couldn't imagine the unhappiness Caroline was steeped in while living in such an adorable, cheerful room.

They left Caroline's room, and at the end of the hall she entered a huge master suite with striking black and white decor.

"Your suite, no doubt," she said, and Will grinned.

"You're getting to know me."

"More a process of elimination."

They went downstairs to a playroom where Will held Caroline and read to her. Next they played a board game with her, and while she remained silent and somber, she moved her pieces to play along with them.

"Want Ava to read one of your new books to you?" Will asked when they finished the board game.

Without looking at Ava, Caroline nodded. The three of them sat on a sofa with Caroline between them while Ava read and let Caroline turn the pages.

Giving her a pleasant surprise, Ava realized Caroline was reading with her enough to know when to turn a page without being told. She looked at the child's tiny hands, so dainty and frail. Caroline smelled sweet, something that held a hint of apples, and her hair was shiny. Ava could see why Will loved her so much and was doing what he could for her.

By the time Ava finished both books, dinner was served by Will's chef, who then disappeared back into the kitchen.

After dinner they played more games with Caroline and then walked outside to sit near the pool.

"Will, this is grand," she said, looking at a covered area with an outdoor stainless-steel kitchen and a patio with upholstered furniture. "You have another kitchen and living room out here. This is incredible."

"It's comfortable like the rest of the house," he said. They talked while Caroline sat at a desk to paint and draw pictures. When she finished, Will praised each picture. Rosalyn arrived to get Caroline ready for bed and the two left.

"She's precious, Will. I can see why you worry so about her."

"She's shut away in her own world where I can't get through to her. No one can."

"Why don't you leave her in my care tomorrow?" Ava suggested. "I've never dealt with a child in this situation before, but I need to get to know her before I talk to the likely tutors."

"Fine. If you're ready for that. If you want just half a day, let me know. If at any point it isn't going well, Rosalyn will be here, so summon her."

"You can give Rosalyn the day off and let me take care of Caroline. We'll be fine."

"I'm sure you will, but you're unaccustomed to that kind of responsibility and a child can wear you down."

She smiled. "I don't think Caroline will."

He stood. "If you'll excuse me, I'll go see Caroline. If I'm home, I always read to her before she goes to bed for the night."

"Of course."

He left and Ava turned to watch him walk away. He'd been telling her the truth about his devotion to Caroline—when he was home he read to her at night. Another plus in Ava's view of him.

Taking the stairs two at a time, Will hurried to Caroline's room. Rosalyn was brushing Caroline's long black hair. His heart felt squeezed that he was here when it should be his brother Adam with her.

"Rosalyn, I'll read to her and I'll call you when I'm ready to go back downstairs."

"Yes, sir," Rosalyn said, looking at Caroline in the mirror. "How pretty you look, Caroline. Here's Uncle Will."

As Rosalyn left the room, Caroline turned to look at him. He wondered if anyone would ever be able to reach her, and if he would ever stop hurting over the tragedy in her life. "You do look so pretty, Caroline." He picked her up. "I'll read to you. You find the book you want, okay?"

She looked at the bookcase as he approached it and set her on her feet. She smelled sweet, fresh and clean, a faint lilac scent left from soap. Her pink pajamas covered in kittens were soft. She touched a book and he pulled it out.

"Ah, good choice," he said, picking her up again and holding the book. He carried her to the rocker to sit with her on his lap.

"Caroline, my friend Miss Ava would like to spend the day with you tomorrow. I'll be home, but I'll be in my office some of the time. Will this be all right with you?"

She gazed at him solemnly and nodded.

"Good. She wants to help you with your reading and she's trying to find a reading tutor for you."

As Caroline focused her big brown eyes on him, he marveled at the length and thickness of her lashes.

"Caroline, Miss Ava has sad moments sometimes because she has lost someone she loved just as you have. She was married, but her husband is no longer alive and there are times this makes her sad."

Caroline gazed at him wide-eyed and solemn. How much did she understand? Did she feel any sympathy or a bond with Ava?

"Now let's look at this book you picked about the brave puppy and the rescued kitten."

He held Caroline, rocking her as he read to her, his mind wandering to Ava and back to Caroline. Halfway through the book Caroline's breathing deepened. He continued reading a few more pages until he saw her dark lashes on her cheeks. He carried the sleeping child to bed and covered her lightly, brushing a kiss on her cheek and standing over her.

"Adam, I'm sorry," he whispered, hurting and feeling helpless, something he was unaccustomed to in his life.

Ava looked around to see Will walk up and pull a chair close to hers.

"Sorry to leave you so long. Caroline is asleep now and Rosalyn is with her."

"How many nannies has she had?

"Actually, Rosalyn is the only nanny we've had. She was her nanny when Adam was alive. Rosalyn had fifteen years' experience, plus her own kids and grandkids. She had great references."

"I'm surprised she didn't become a substitute mother to Caroline, someone your niece would relate to emotionally."

"Rosalyn has tried—sometimes I think too hard. She comes on too strong and it makes Caroline withdraw. Rosalyn means well and loves Caroline. She's very good to her. I told her your plan to stay with Caroline tomorrow, and I'll be home, so I gave her the day off. Still want to do that?"

"Yes, I do. I'd like to get to know her. I don't expect to need you," she said, smiling at him.

"I know, but just in case."

"We'll be fine, and I appreciate your concern. It's only a day, perhaps two at the most." She gazed into his dark eyes and could tell he was assessing her, trying to decide whether she could take care of Caroline or not. "By the way, you were right about her ability to read. The two books I read to her today are both beginner reading level and I know she can read them. I realized after a few pages she knew when to turn the page without being told, so she had to be reading along with me. Then I began to do things to make certain, like pausing on the last line and looking at the picture. Little things, but she had to be reading with me to know, because otherwise she would turn before I indicated I was through."

"That's a plus, but not too great if she won't participate at school."

"Let's see what happens this summer. Time helps some on loss."

He focused on her again. "Sorry about yours. I told Caroline. As always, I got no reaction from her except a stare, but she knows about your husband."

"I don't know if she'll bond, but I feel a tie of sorts with her. As for my coping, I keep busy and am involved with children and coworkers, so I don't think about it as much."

"Maybe you need to get out and socialize more," he said.

She smiled. "I socialize plenty. And I know you do. If there's someone in your life and you want to see her tomorrow evening, go right ahead."

His eyes twinkled. "Don't try to get rid of me. There's no one in my life and the only woman I'm interested in seeing tomorrow night is you. Aside from Caroline, I have a life. Go to dinner with me Friday night and I'll show you."

Her heart skipped a beat. For the first time since Ethan's loss, she was tempted to go out with someone else. She wanted to accept, yet it would be folly to get involved with Will. He was a heartbreaker, with a reputation for going from woman to woman. Right now she needed no such distraction in her life. He was a sizzling attraction that she'd fought steadily through the afternoon and evening.

She was not complicating her life by seeing him beyond these two days. The physical reaction she had to him had shaken her. She didn't want to risk succumbing to an affair with Will because it would be brief and meaningless to him. A casual affair was the last thing she ever wanted in her life. With Will, she suspected a date would ultimately lead to an affair. The best course was to go home and never see Will Delaney again.

"Thank you, but I think I should stay right here Friday night."

"Scared to go out with me?"

"Definitely," she said, smiling at him. "I don't need a complication in my life. I'm here only to help Caroline. As quiet as she is, she's adorable, Will. In her own unobtrusive way, she wraps herself around your heart. I can see why you're concerned."

"Looks like I have two females to win over now," he said quietly, and her pulse jumped a notch.

"Stop flirting, Will," she said, smiling at him.

"I can't. I want to take you out."

"It isn't going to happen. Your brother must have been a great parent," she said, determined to get the subject changed.

"He was, and he loved her beyond measure."

"Were you and your brother close?"

"Yes, the closest brother. I'm close with my other brothers and some friends I've known all my life."

"I noticed the rodeo memorabilia in your room. Do you still ride?"

"I haven't for the past two years. Mostly because of lack of time."

They talked about their friends and their lives until she realized the hour was late. Standing, she smiled at him as he came to his feet.

"It's past my bedtime. Plus, I haven't taken time to unpack. I should go."

"I'll go up with you in case you've forgotten the way."

"Have you ever thought about getting Caroline a puppy?" Ava asked as they headed upstairs

"No, it never occurred to me," he admitted, glancing at her. "I don't know why I didn't think of that, or why it wasn't suggested earlier by someone."

"It may not be something she wants."

"It would be a little puppy to take care of. How could she resist loving one if it has a good disposition? When we were kids, my brothers and I had dogs. That's a good idea," he said. "I should have thought of a dog myself."

She nodded. "A puppy might elicit a few laughs from her. Puppies are hard to resist. They do have sharp teeth though, and that can be a drawback for little kids."

"I'll get someone to check into which breeds are good with children. Big or little," he mused. "Seems like little might be easier."

"It probably would be. Talk to a veterinarian."

"That's a great idea. I need to keep you around." Startled, she glanced at him and smiled when she saw his smile and realized he was teasing her.

They reached her suite and he entered with her, switching on lights and taking her arm. "Come look around and see if you need anything."

"I'm sure I won't."

He turned her to face him. "I'll be forever grateful to the principal who gave me your name."

He stood close and his hands were on her arms. Her heart raced, and at the moment she was no longer thinking of him as Caroline's uncle, a man with a problem who needed her help. Instead, she could only see the handsome, sexy man who was inches away and holding her lightly. When he looked at her mouth, she couldn't get her breath and wondered if he could hear her heart pounding. She wanted to wrap her arms around him to kiss him. Her desire shocked her.

"I think you're bringing me back into the world and I'm not certain I'm ready," she whispered.

"You're ready," he said in a husky voice. "I can see it in your eyes." He leaned closer and bent down to brush her lips with his.

The moment his mouth touched hers, she closed her eyes. Her heart thudded. She had not been kissed by a man since Ethan—six long years ago. Her pulse roared in her ears.

Will's breath was warm. He brushed her lips again and then his mouth settled possessively on hers, hard, demanding, no longer light and tentative.

Her toes curled and her heart pounded. Her body reacted to his kiss from head to toe. She slipped her arms up to wrap them around his neck and hold him, feeling his body hard and warm against hers.

His tongue went deep, thrusting over hers, creating an intimacy they hadn't had and taking them to a different level in their relationship, shifting from business to pleasure, from impersonal to personal. For the moment she wanted him as she had wanted few men in her life. Her reactions to him surprised her. Reasoning stopped while her body and heart ruled.

She held him tightly, kissing him back and feeling his heart pounding with hers.

Even though she had decided to keep her relationship purely professional with him to protect her heart from succumbing to his charm, she couldn't resist his kisses. She had been steeped in grief so long, this was sunshine pouring into a dark night. Somewhere within her conscience a dim voice whispered stop, but she paid no heed. She felt the rough stubble of his whiskers, inhaled his aftershave, savored his mouth.

How long they kissed, she had no idea. Will's hand traveled to her nape, warm, lightly caressing her, and then his hand slipped down her back to her waist, then lower over the curve of her bottom.

Pausing, she looked up at him while he still held her. "We should stop this, Will. It's total foolishness. Risks neither of us want."

"Speak for yourself." His brown eyes blazed and he wound both hands in her hair. "I want you, Ava. I want to know you," he said. "And you like being kissed. Your response sets me on fire," he whispered, pulling her close again and then kissing away any answer she might have.

Again, a wave of desire swept her and she held him tightly, kissing him, relishing the feel of his hard body against hers. She tingled from head to toe, heat pooling in her. Special kisses when they shouldn't be. Or was it simply so long since she had been held by a man? Thoughts spun away and she was lost in his kisses, returning them passionately until she had to stop.

"Will," she said, trying to get some firmness to her breathless voice. "You need to go."

Desire blazed in his dark eyes, making her racing heart pound faster. He wrapped his fingers in her hair to hold her head. "For now," he said. He released her, leaving the room and closing the door behind him.

Immobile, she stared at the closed door, but all she saw was Will. Locks of his dark hair falling over his forehead, his gaze boring into her, his mouth red from kisses. Had she made a giant mistake by succumbing?

Not succumbing—she had kissed him passionately in return, wanting more. It was a good thing she had only two days here. Will was a sexy, appealing man. Caroline, an adorable child. Both could wind around her heartstrings until she was bound in unbreakable shackles with a man who had no intention of a serious relationship and a child who wasn't hers and would soon go out of her life forever.

Each event would lead to heartbreak.

Three

In the morning, Ava stepped into the kitchen to find Will's chef working at a counter.

Short, stocky, an apron around his waist, the man paused and smiled. "Good morning."

Before she could answer, Will entered the room and for seconds as her gaze met his, she forgot all else. In a knit shirt and chinos, he looked casual, more appealing than ever. "Good morning," he said, gazing warmly at her. He touched her arm lightly and his tone became brisk.

"Ava, meet my very fine chef, Rainey Powers. Rainey, meet Miss Ava Barton, a teacher who will be working with Caroline.

"Good morning," she said, smiling at the man who had thick red curly hair and big brown eyes.

"What's your preference for breakfast, Ava?" Will asked. "Rainey has a specialty—omelets. If you would like one, just tell him what kind."

"I usually have some fruit."

"You can have that, too," Will said, "but don't pass up a chance to have one of his amazing omelets."

After she decided on spinach and mushroom, Will led her to a casual dining area overlooking the veranda and pool.

"You look gorgeous today," he said, pulling a chair out for her, his eyes on her blue cotton shirt and matching pants.

"Thank you," she said, aware of how close he stood. When his gaze lowered to her mouth, her heartbeat quickened. He sat across the table where a newspaper lay folded neatly and his coffee cup was half full.

He picked up a pitcher. "Orange juice?"

"Yes, please," she said. "I'm surprised Caroline isn't here."

"Occasionally, she sleeps late."

"Maybe she's dreading the day and being with someone new."

He paused in his pouring. "Maybe. You'll never know. I have no idea what runs through her mind. Good or bad. She accepts everything, comments on nothing. It's that total unresponsiveness that will hurt her in school."

"Have you considered home schooling or a special school?"

"I'm afraid with home schooling she would become more withdrawn and antisocial. I don't want a special school. At least not for now. I'd rather try to find someone who can break through the guard she keeps. If I ever do, I think all the withdrawal will vanish."

"I imagine you're hopeful with each thing and person you've tried," she said, watching him nod. "Don't get too hopeful with me. I'm out of my element here. I have never worked with a child who had problems like this."

"I understand. But no one has higher recommendations than you in this field. I know a happy little girl is locked away somewhere inside her. I want her back again."

"I'll do my best with her."

"I'm sure you will. How did you sleep?" he asked, changing the topic abruptly.

"Fine," she answered, yet her cheeks grew warm because she instantly thought about their kisses.

He looked amused. "About as well as I did."

"I met your housekeeper in the upstairs hall this morning."

"Edwina. My staff are all here on Tuesdays and Fridays and then some of them are just here when I ask them to be or when I'm in town."

"So you travel a lot."

"Yes. I hear Rosalyn." He stood, and in seconds Rosalyn and Caroline walked through the door.

"Good morning," Will said, greeting them both and picking up Caroline to hug her. The girl's pigtails swung. She wrapped her arm around his neck and hugged him in return, Ava noticed.

"Rosalyn, go give your order to Rainey and then come join us. He knows Caroline's. I already have places set."

As Rosalyn left, Will set Caroline in one of the chairs.

"So Rosalyn joins you for breakfast. That's nice."

"Rosalyn is like a relative. Actually, all of my staff have worked for me long enough now that I feel like they're my family. And you'll have to adjust your view of me again."

"I shouldn't have told you what I expected." He was one continual surprise, and she promised herself never to prejudge anyone again. "The articles and press about you just present a different type person—not quite so down-to-earth and caring. I'm impressed," she said.

"Good. That's a step in the right direction."

Rosalyn joined them and conversation became impersonal, polite, chatty among the three adults, swirling around the silent child as if she didn't exist.

After breakfast they divided up, Rosalyn leaving, Will heading to his office while Ava went to the upstairs playroom with Caroline. "Come to my room, Caroline. I want to get a package I brought. I have a new game for you."

Obediently, Caroline followed and Ava retrieved a large

colorful sack that held gift bags and books. She pulled out a gift to hand to Caroline, seeing no spark of interest in Caroline's eyes.

"This is for you," Ava said, setting it in front of the girl, who glanced up at Ava and then looked at the sack. After pulling out tissue paper, she picked up a game that she turned in her hands.

"Thank you," she whispered politely and set it on the floor.

"I'll show you how to play it. All right?"

Caroline nodded.

"Before we do, here's another little present I got for you."

Caroline opened a small gift sack and once again tossed aside blue and red tissue paper to reveal a small brown teddy bear.

"Thank you," she said, looking intently at it.

"You're welcome. Now I'll show you how to play this game. Let's go to the playroom."

In the playroom, Ava put her things on a sofa and turned to Caroline. "I think you'll like this game. We can sit on the floor to play." Ava kicked off her shoes while she got out cards.

"See these, Caroline," she said, glad when she noticed that the girl still held the small bear. Was she grasping at straws about Caroline's responses the way Will did? "Each card has a letter. We're going to place them all facedown," Ava added, putting cards facedown in a row. "Then we'll take turns. Each of us can turn over two cards and the object of the game is to match the letters. If you turn over an A and a C, the next time if you turn over an A, try to find the matching A again. The one with the most pairs of matching letters wins the game. Is that clear?"

When Caroline nodded, Ava continued, "As soon as I put out all the cards, you can go first. Do you want to help me put the cards facedown?"

Caroline shook her head no, so Ava placed the cards in silence. As soon as she finished, she told Caroline to go ahead.

During the game, Ava glanced around to see Will standing in the doorway. As soon as she looked up, he left and she wondered how long he had been there.

Other than her silence, Ava thought she could be playing with any first grader she had known, and Caroline was just going into kindergarten.

Midmorning they paused for a snack and watched a short movie Ava had brought. Still holding the teddy, Caroline watched intently, never laughing or even smiling at the funny spots, and Ava didn't think she was going to get to know the solemn little girl even a degree better. Ava's satisfaction over Caroline's abilities with letters and words was offset by her growing frustration at being unable to get a glimmer of emotional response.

The person who would get the job of working with Caroline had a big task ahead.

By eleven o'clock Ava asked Caroline if she would like to swim and Caroline nodded. Rosalyn had told Ava that she had laid out Caroline's swimsuits and she could get one on by herself.

At the pool Ava shed the oversize T-shirt she had worn and her flip-flops while she watched Caroline go in cautiously.

Wondering whether Will would show up, Ava was acutely conscious of her new swimsuit—a conservative navy one-piece. The water was just cool enough to be enticing, and the circular pool was beautiful with a waterfall and a fountain.

She relaxed when Will did not show, nor did she see any sign of him.

Caroline splashed in the shallow end and then when Ava asked, Caroline showed her how she could swim, tread water and float.

Eventually, they lay on inflatable mattresses, looking at billowing thunderheads against a deep blue sky.

Will kept his word and disappeared for the day. By the time Caroline stretched out for quiet time in her room, she had a stack of books beside her.

Ava lay next to her.

"All right, which one do you want me to read to you first?"

Caroline handed her a book.

"Teddy's New House," she read. "You turn pages, Caroline."

Halfway through the book, Ava stopped reading before the last word on the page. "Do you know that word?" she asked.

Caroline looked a long time at the word and nodded.

"Will you read it to me? I would like that so much," Ava said quietly, holding her breath and wondering if she had alienated Caroline further.

There was a long silence and Ava waited, finally turning the page and reading the next one. Just before she reached the end, she paused and waited, finally reading the word. She did the same on the next pages. She was on the next to the last page when she paused again before reading the last word.

Caroline whispered, "Shoe."

"Thank you, Caroline." Ava's heart skipped a beat when she heard Caroline's faint voice. "Some things are just hard for us to do, but we can do them."

As far as she was concerned, Ava saw the slight response as a tiny victory, one she didn't care to push, so she didn't ask Caroline to read anything else aloud.

The day passed with Ava learning a little about Caroline's typical day and her responses. Ava suspected Caroline's behavior wasn't very different with Rosalyn or Will. Ava couldn't feel much closer to the child because of the wall Caroline kept around herself. Will had been good to leave them alone—another surprise with him, because she had expected him to hang around and continue flirting. It was better he hadn't, but she missed seeing him.

It wasn't until almost dinner that he joined them in the pool. Ava didn't see him coming until he was at the edge of the deep end. Her pulse jumped when she saw him. He was deeply tanned. His broad, sculpted chest tapered to a small waist, tight muscles on his flat stomach. He wore black-and-white patterned swim trunks. He made a flying leap and landed in the water with a loud splash, causing Caroline to smile.

He bobbed up by her, lifting her and then letting her splash down, but he held her the whole time.

"Want to do that again?" he asked her, holding her up again, and she smiled, nodding.

With a surprised expression he glanced over her head at Ava and then lifted Caroline higher to let her splash into the water again.

They played and he gave his full attention to Caroline, glancing once at Ava to say hello.

Later as Caroline splashed nearby, he swam close to Ava. When he bobbed up almost touching her, Ava's heartbeat sped, a reaction she couldn't control and one that happened too often with him. "Hi."

She smiled at him. "Hi."

"You know why I've been giving her all my attention."

"Of course, and you should."

"Caroline smiling at me like that—I think you brought that on. She hasn't done that before with me. I was right about you. You are good with her."

"Thank you. You may give me too much credit," she said. "I did get her to read one word aloud today."

Something flickered in the depths of his dark eyes. "I'm going to do some arm twisting and see if you'll stay this coming week. We'll talk about it later."

"Will, the people I'm recommending will be better than I am in working with her."

Smiling, he swam away to join Caroline, and she guessed she was in for a struggle with a man totally accustomed to getting his way.

After the swim, they ate dinner with Caroline and then played games until Will took Caroline upstairs to get her ready for bed. After half an hour he reappeared. "I came down to get you. She wants you to read a story to her if you will. I volunteered you, and she nodded."

"Sure, I'd be happy to," Ava said, going with him, gratified that Caroline wanted her to read.

"Rosalyn called and she'll be here in about an hour. Ava, you've gotten closer than anyone else except my brothers and me. Actually, you're getting more response out of her than my brothers do. Even Rosalyn doesn't get as much response as you'd think. Rosalyn gets more than my brothers, but not a lot."

"It's so slight. Don't read much into it."

"As far as I'm concerned, it's a breakthrough. Her teachers have gotten no responses."

"I think you're grasping at straws, Will," Ava said gently.

"We'll see."

They had reached Caroline's suite to find her sitting on the floor playing with miniature dolls and the small brown teddy bear beside a doll house.

"Time for a story and bed," Will said. "Get your book for Miss Ava and climb into bed. She'll read it to you and I'll be back to tuck you in."

In minutes Ava lay beside Caroline, reading while Caroline turned the pages again. She noticed that Caroline leaned close this time, pressing against Ava's side, something she had not done before. As she read, Ava put her arm lightly around Caroline.

They finished. "Do you want another story until your Uncle Will comes back?"

Caroline shook her head no, so Ava stood beside the bed, tucking Caroline with the sheet beneath her chin. "It's been a fun day, Caroline. I'll be here one more day. We'll probably do about the same thing tomorrow. Maybe we can get your uncle to take us to a bookstore and you can get a new book. If you want to."

Big brown eyes looked up at her as Caroline stared without any response. "Do you hurt?" Caroline whispered.

Caroline asked the question so softly, Ava almost did not hear her. Startled, she guessed the question was not about physical pain at the moment, but about the loss of her husband. "Yes. It comes and it goes, but he's always there in my heart."

Caroline looked down at the sheet and twisted it in her small fingers. "I don't have a mommy and daddy. I used to have Daddy."

"I know," Ava said. "It hurts, but there are other people you can love and they love you. Your Uncle Will loves you so, so much."

Big brown eyes met her gaze again and Ava's heart lurched over the silent world into which Caroline had locked herself. Ava tried to avoid intruding on Caroline, but at the sight of Caroline's solemn expression, Ava could not resist leaning down to hug her lightly. "You are so loved, Caroline."

Caroline slipped an arm around Ava's neck and held on for a moment. When her arm slipped away, Ava released her. "You're a brave little girl," she said.

Caroline looked away and Ava felt the closeness vanish, suspecting Caroline was withdrawing back into her shell.

"Nighty-night time," Will said cheerfully, entering the room. "One more story from me if you want and then it's sleepy time. Miss Rosalyn is back and she'll be here soon."

"Good night, Caroline," Ava said with a smile and she turned away with a glance at Will.

Shaken by the moments with Caroline, she went downstairs to wait in the family room. It was another half hour before Will appeared. He swept into the room, crossing the space in long strides to pull her up and hug her tightly. "You are a miracle worker," he said. "I came into the room when she hugged you. I stepped out and came back because I didn't want to break the moment."

"Will," she said, extricating herself and smiling. "Slow down. A little gain maybe. A baby step."

He held her arms as he gazed down at her. Her racing pulse was half because of the moments with Caroline and half because of Will standing close and holding her.

"It's huge, Ava. I've tried so many things, so many experts and nobody could get anywhere."

"I think it's because she feels a tie since I lost my husband."

"Maybe, but she's had people around who have lost someone and kids around who have lost parents and she wouldn't respond to them at all. It's more than that."

"I'm surprised the kids didn't reach her."

"They didn't. Maybe everyone came on too strong. I notice you're pretty low-key with her."

"There's no magic formula and I don't know why, but she's responding slightly to me."

"It isn't slight. For her to hug you is huge."

"You're making so much out of so little, I'm scared to tell you anything else."

"Now you have to. What else?"

"Just don't get carried away. She asked me tonight if I hurt." For an instant he stared at her and she wondered if she would regret telling him. "Will, don't blow everything out of proportion. I see big hope for your tutor because the woman I have in mind should be wonderful with Caroline."

"Let's sit. What did you tell her?" he asked, taking her arm and moving to the sofa to sit close, facing her. Their knees touched and his hand still rested on her arm.

She told him about the brief moment she had had with Caroline.

"You did it. I knew you could," he said. "You've gotten through to her."

"Will, stop making something colossal out of this. It's a tiny step, a baby step in the right direction."

He framed her face with his hands. "We've tried so much. You should see the list of people I've had work with her and the play groups I've put her into."

"Maybe she just wasn't ready and time has passed and now she is," Ava said, her voice breathless. His hands were on her cheeks and he sat close, his eyes blazing with emotion.

"I'm overjoyed, Ava. Maybe I'm clutching at straws, but straws are more than I've had in the past. This is real hope. She communicated with you, however briefly. She interacted with you."

His gaze dropped to her mouth and her heart pounded. He leaned down to kiss her hard and she responded to him, knowing he kissed her with emotion and joy over his feelings for his niece. As his kiss changed, he lifted her onto his lap. A half day with him tomorrow. It wouldn't last, so what did a few kisses hurt? She wrapped her arm more tightly around his neck and kissed him passionately, forgetting everything except Will, who was exciting, sexy, temporarily changing her life.

When she withdrew, his breathing was as ragged as hers. He stared at her as if he had never seen her before, his gaze roaming over her features while he combed his hand through her hair. "You'll continue to spend time with her tomorrow, won't you?"

"Yes, but I've really learned what I wanted to know—who would make the best tutor for her. I told her you might take us to a bookstore and she can pick out some books."

"Sounds great. I should go tell Rosalyn that she can have

another day off, so if she wants to make plans this evening, she can. I'll be right back."

He left and she watched him go, looking at his long legs, remembering him in his swimsuit and thinking about his kisses. Tonight was the last night with him—a good thing. No one-night stands, either. It would take her a long time to forget him and his niece. She was going to miss Caroline. The little girl in her quiet way was lovable.

In minutes Will was back. "She's glad for another day to catch up on some things, so everyone is happy and I'm sure Caroline will be." He sat close on the sofa again. "Want anything to drink? Tea, pop, wine, beer, milk, margaritas, rum... I have a full bar."

"A glass of iced tea would be good," she said, standing to go to the kitchen with him. She watched as he fixed her a tall glass, gave her some sliced lemon and got out a cold beer for himself. He motioned toward a sofa in the far side of the kitchen where there was an adjoining sitting room.

When she sat on the sofa, Will sat close beside her. He raised his drink. "Here's to miracles."

She smiled patiently and touched his glass with hers. "Something to dream about."

"No dream today. I told you—you have no idea what we've gone through with none of the experts getting that much reaction from her."

"Now that I've met Caroline, I plan to contact Becky first because she's the best choice as tutor. She's free for the rest of the summer and she lives in driving distance of Dallas so she can stay or drive back and forth, either one. Now I can tell Becky more about Caroline and know what I'm talking about. I think you'll like Becky."

"Ava, I've thought over who I want to hire," he said, setting his beer on a coaster on the table. "I didn't come up with my plans tonight or even earlier today. I promise."

She set her drink on the nearby table. "You don't approve of Becky? You read all I sent you, didn't you?"

"Yes, I did. One person stands out."

"And who is that?"

He took her hands. "I'd like to hire you to tutor Caroline this summer."

Four

Even though Ava had suspected this request was coming, it still surprised her. She thought of Caroline and felt torn.

"Will, thank you for your faith in me. Caroline is adorable and I think she can be helped. She's a precious child." Will was desperate, and she had already gotten to know him well enough that she disliked disappointing him. She hated even more hurting Caroline, although his niece would never know about his offer or her rejection.

"If you feel that way, don't rush to answer me. Think about it tonight and give me an answer tomorrow. You see the situation here, so you know what we're like and where you'd live and what you'd be doing. Just give it some thought."

"When we first met I told you my plans. I've received my doctorate. I intend to open my own school where I can hire the teachers I want and include some of my teaching methods with my books in the curriculum."

"I appreciate your ambition. All I'm asking you to do is postpone your plans a little," he said, leaning slightly closer.

"Opening my own school has been my dream since I was a student aide in high school and helped in a reading program."

"An admirable dream," he remarked. His dark gaze consumed her and her heartbeat raced. She had no intention of letting him derail all her plans. She took a deep breath, ready to launch into a refusal.

"You're perfect to work with Caroline and it's already June," he said before she could speak. "It would be the rest of this month, July and only part of August until shortly before school begins. Not quite three full months actually. It would be a three-month delay in your plans at most."

"I don't want to put off my dream. I'm really not a private tutor. When you meet and interview Becky, I think you'll agree that she's the best person for the job, and I'm sure Caroline will like her."

He reached in a pocket and brought out a piece of paper, which he unfolded.

She was tempted to refuse to even look at it. She suspected it would be an exorbitant sum of several thousand dollars, like the amount he was paying her for the two days in Dallas.

"I figured you would turn me down, so I've thought about what might induce you to stay. Don't give me an answer now. Promise me you'll take this and think about it tonight."

"Will, I know what I want to do," she persisted. "This isn't the place for me to get sidetracked, because it's more than just taking a job for the summer. This involves a child and you— It could be complicated." The man wasn't accustomed to hearing no, but he was going to have to adjust.

As if he hadn't heard her, he continued, "Just remember, a little over three months would not be a big delay in your plans, yet it would give you some finances for your school." He held the paper out to her. "Here's what I will pay you if you work through the summer months with Caroline."

While she could use the money, she didn't want to look at the amount and be tempted. Will Delaney was temptation in every way. She didn't want to spend almost three months under the same roof with him, didn't want to change her plans because it could be a far bigger delay once summer was over and everyone got busy with the school year.

"Will, I'm sorry, but I've already commenced several things. I have a real estate agent looking for a location. I'm working on getting grants."

"Give me half a chance here," he said quietly. "You can at least look at what I'm offering."

"It won't matter," she said, growing slightly more annoyed because he still held her hand and had the paper in front of her.

"Take it, Ava," he said in a more commanding tone. "Otherwise you'll always wonder."

Certain in another few minutes he would just tell her, she took the paper in exasperation. "Will, this is just ridiculous for you to be so stubborn."

"I'm not the only one being stubborn. You can at least look at my figures and my offer."

"Will, I understand how you—" Frowning, Ava held the paper closer to study the figures he had written. Her gaze ran over the amounts several times. Stunned, she looked at one half million dollars to tutor for the summer and another half million if Caroline came out of her withdrawal.

Ava's astonished gaze jumped to meet his. "You can't be serious," she whispered.

"I'm absolutely in earnest," he replied. "You'll live here. You'll be off on Saturdays and Sundays. I can have someone fly you home on weekends if you want. I want you to tutor Caroline so she can go into kindergarten this fall and fit in. Hopefully, you might get her out of her shell. You already have a great start."

"This is an astronomical figure," Ava said. Her eyes narrowed. "What else do you expect from me?"

"Nothing personal," he replied, appearing slightly amused

by her question. "Although you know I won't stop flirting, and I'll ask you out."

She opened her mouth and then closed it and gave him another questioning glance. "This is way too much money for such a job."

"I think you can help Caroline. It's worth that to me if you will try. I've already spent a fortune with no results. I've had doctors, counselors, shrinks, tutors—all to no avail. I've been told no one can work as well with children as you can."

"Thanks. That's nice, but I don't know that it's completely accurate."

"Don't give me an answer now. Think about it and think about what that money can do for you and your school and your students."

Their gazes locked. Physically aware of him, she was stunned by the staggering amount of money he offered her. Now she had to give his offer consideration. How could she turn down half a million and a chance for a million if all worked out? She wouldn't have to worry about grants. She could buy land and a building without a struggle for financing.

Anger and dismay churned in her. He had demolished her well-laid plans. He would derail her dreams to try to get what he wanted. He had already admitted he would flirt and ask her out. Her resistance to his charm was almost nonexistent. How much would she complicate her life? If he went to such lengths to get her to work for him, how persistent would he be in trying to get her in his bed?

She stood to break the mesmerizing spell he wove and to get to herself to think clearly, but there was only one answer to give him now.

He came to his feet the moment she stood.

"I need to turn in for tonight. I'll think about this, of course," she said, feeling overwhelmed and still stunned. She could not turn him down now, not with this kind of money.

But she wasn't going to capitulate the instant he waved a paycheck at her.

He took her arm. "I'll see you to your room."

She didn't protest because she was lost in thought, but then she realized what he had said and that he walked beside her.

They were silent until she reached the door of her suite, where she turned to face him. "You barely know me. I've only known Caroline for one day. You don't really know whether I'll be this much help to Caroline or not."

"She likes you. You made her smile when no one else has. I'm willing to take the chance. It's worth the risk to me to have you try. I'll never miss the money, and even if I did, if it helps Caroline, it's worth it to me."

"It doesn't bother you to wreck someone else's plans?"

"I haven't wrecked your plans, Ava. The money I'm offering will help you get that school months or years faster than you would without it. Also, you said you would start with only first and second grade because of limited funds. Now you won't be quite so limited. I'm not tearing up your plans—I'm aiding them. You're free to make a choice."

"That I am," she said. "It's been an interesting day. I'll give you an answer tomorrow."

She was angry with his high-handed methods, stunned by the amount, shaken that she could earn that much money in just under three months. Weighing more heavily were the problems she would have with Will and Caroline. She didn't want to fall in love with Will, and that's what an affair would mean. An affair for her would be an affair of the heart that needed commitment and real love.

When Will's gaze lowered to her mouth, Ava held her breath. Her lips parted, tingled. She wanted his kisses while at the same time she didn't. "Good night, Will," she said, turning blindly and stepping into her suite, closing the door swiftly behind her.

She crossed the room and sat on a chair to stare at the figures scribbled boldly on the paper. Half a million to stay and work with Caroline for the next three months. Three months—a brief postponement of her dreams that would be more than made up when she could open a school, fully funded.

She could not possibly turn down the opportunity for the half million. If she connected and Caroline responded to her, there would be another half million. Ava stared at the paper and the figures danced before her. She had never been a therapist, yet she knew she could work well with the girl—academically and emotionally.

If she didn't succeed, well, she had warned Will about her inexperience in this area. Three months. In those three months if she bonded with Caroline, she might love the little girl with all her heart and it would hurt to leave. And she would leave when the summer ended. She had a life and a career to pursue. Could she resist Will for the entire summer?

She leaned back in the chair, staring at the ceiling. *Tell him no,* came a small voice in her mind. *Just say no and walk away.*

Only she couldn't. The chance for a half million or, if dreams came true, a million, didn't come along in most lifetimes. If she turned down Will's offer, she would be looking back forever. Particularly if financing became difficult. She had planned on grants, investors and relying on tuition. Now she would not be dependent on anything.

"Will Delaney, the demanding Delaney," she said aloud, her thoughts jumping to their kisses until she was hot, tingly and filled with desire.

Impatiently, she stood to get ready for bed. Later, lying in the darkness, the turn of events and the amount of money being dangled before her kept her awake until almost dawn when she fell into a fitful sleep.

Saturday, Ava showered and dressed carefully in a navy shirt and slacks—casual but professional. When she walked into the kitchen, Will sat outside on the veranda at a table. He read an iPad on the table in front of him. He was in chinos, a black knit shirt and Western boots. Her pulse jumped merely at the sight of him and she had one more moment of reluctance. She had to give him an answer, and as far as she could see, there was only one reply.

He stood and smiled, approval lighting his eyes as his gaze swept over her. "Good morning. You look great."

"Thank you," she answered coolly, knowing she should be thrilled and eager when he made such a large offer, but she wanted him to know he couldn't push her around.

He walked up to her and her pulse drummed faster when he placed his hands on her shoulders.

"Come sit and I'll get your breakfast. Want coffee and orange juice now?"

"I can help myself," she said, picking up a china cup.

When Ava was seated and had breakfast in front of her, Will also sat and sipped black coffee. "Have you thought over my offer?"

"Of course," she replied, meeting his gaze. "And I accept. It's an offer I can't refuse, as you well knew. I think you expect miracles."

"I think you can do miracles," he answered quietly, his eyes flaring with triumph. It added to her annoyance that he was so confident and able to get his way easily.

"Go to dinner with me tonight. I want to celebrate hiring you for the summer."

"Maybe we should make some rules from the first," she answered. "You said there were no demands on me other than where Caroline is concerned."

Again, amusement flared in his expression so slightly, yet she had no doubt that's what he felt. "That's correct, but I thought you might enjoy a night out and to get to see a little of Dallas."

"I've been to Dallas before," she answered. "Thank you,

but I'd like to keep my personal life separate. I don't care to go out unless it is something involving Caroline."

"Whatever you want," he said smoothly and her insides tightened. She would love to go out with him, but she wasn't going down that road.

"If possible, I should return home today, get my things in order and make arrangements to be gone for the next three months. I'd like a week to get ready and return a week from tomorrow to begin work. How will that fit with your schedule?"

"Fine, I'll take you home today. I'd like to tell Caroline the news because I think she'll be pleased."

"I think you're reading much more into a relationship between your niece and me than there really is," she persisted.

"Time will tell," he said, smiling at her. He reached across the table to squeeze her hand. "Thanks for doing this, Ava."

The contact made her tingle and the warmth in his voice heightened her reaction to him. Three months in the same house with a charismatic, seductive man. That might turn out to be as big a challenge as working with Caroline.

"There is no way I can turn down your offer, but I can't give you any guarantees. I've never done this before, tutored long-term in a home with a child with problems as deep as Caroline has. I'll do what I can."

"That's all I ask."

Hours later, when she unlocked the door to her condo, Will stepped inside. He took her arm lightly and turned her to face him.

As she looked up at him, her breathing altered.

"This doesn't have anything to do with your working for me," he said in a husky voice. "It's simply a man and a woman he's attracted to." Her lips parted as she drew a deep breath. He leaned down to kiss her, covering her mouth with his before she could answer.

Her heart thudded and she stood still, unresponsive for a heartbeat, and then she melted against his hard frame. She wrapped her arms around his neck and kissed him in return. His fingers wrapped in her hair a few moments as he leaned over her and kissed her passionately.

His tongue thrust deeply into her mouth. His kisses were more devastating than before. Desire blazed, threatening her peaceful world. She stepped back. "This isn't part of the bargain, Will. It just can't be. I've got my life all lined up and you've already turned it upside down for the summer. I don't want a big emotional upheaval on top of that."

"I don't, either," he said solemnly. "It's kisses and wanting to dance with you and hold you, nothing deep or involved. Get back in the world, Ava. You're too full of life to withdraw into a shell."

"You barely know me or what I do or how I am."

"I'm beginning to know you, and I know that much about you already," he whispered, showering kisses on her temple and cheek, brushing them lightly across her lips. She closed her eyes and in seconds they kissed again until she stopped him.

"I have to say goodbye now, Will. I'll see you a week from Sunday afternoon."

He smiled at her, running his fingers lightly on her throat. "See you at three next Sunday."

She watched him climb back into the limo and leave. Dazed, she moved through her condo, feeling as if she had been caught up in a whirlwind and now dropped back to earth.

She got out her iPad to check her calendar and begin listing what she needed to do before she saw Will again on Sunday. Then she sent a text to her sister. In an hour, Trinity was at the door.

"Tell me what you're doing and where you've been and about William Delaney!" Trinity exclaimed, rushing inside, her sandy curls bouncing. "I brought pizza," she said, waving boxes with enticing smells.

"It's good to see you and to be home," Ava said, smiling, knowing an explosion was coming. "What would you like to drink?" She headed to her small kitchen while Trinity followed and set the pizzas on the table.

"Water. I have veggie blast and artichoke, basil and onion pizza."

"Thanks. Let me pay you."

"My treat, and you talk. What's he like? Does he look like his pictures? Does he have a woman in his life? Is he nice?"

Ava laughed. "Trinity, slow down. One question at a time. He's nicer than I thought he would be. He is more handsome than his pictures," she said, remembering his kisses. "As far as I know there's no woman in his life right now, but I really don't know for sure. He was nice. He has a little niece whose dad was killed in a plane crash, and he's worried about her because she's sort of closed off the world."

"That's dreadful and sad," Trinity said, her smile vanishing. "How old is she?"

"Five." Ava set two glasses of water on the table and told Trinity about Caroline's situation.

Trinity looked horrified. "Poor little thing. So is he going to interview the tutors you recommended?"

Ava braced herself. "No. He's hired me for the summer to work with her."

"You're going to work for him and give up all your plans?" Trinity asked, her eyebrows arching as she stared at Ava.

"Yes. He gave me an incentive."

Trinity squinted her eyes and tilted her head to study her sister. "You didn't fall in love with him, did you?"

"Of course, not," Ava snapped, while a twinge of guilt about the kisses she'd shared with him plagued her. "He made an offer I really couldn't refuse." She withdrew the piece of paper from her purse. "You might want to sit before you read it," she added, bracing again for her sister's reaction.

With one more long look at Ava, Trinity took the paper to read. Her mouth dropped open and she looked up at Ava. "Is this real?"

"Very. I'll have money for my dream and be able to help you and Summer through school."

Trinity looked at the paper again and read it aloud, suddenly screaming as she jumped up and down.

Ava smiled and held out her hand. "Now you see why I postponed my plans until fall. Give me back my paper. I want to keep it."

To Ava's amusement, Trinity reacted in typical fashion and it was an hour before she calmed. They called their youngest sister, Summer, to tell her the change in Ava's plans, and then Ava spent the next several hours with Trinity. The only topics of discussion were Will, Caroline and summer plans.

It was almost nine before Trinity left. Ava felt wound up, filled with excitement, trying to ignore the constant simmering prospect of spending the summer with Will Delaney. To tell someone else about Will's offer, actually show Trinity the amount written by Will, made it seem slightly more real.

At ten, a violin rendition of a Strauss waltz played faintly and she rushed to answer her cell phone to hear Will's voice.

"Did I call too late?"

"Of course not," she answered, her pulse speeding simply over the sound of his voice. She sat in a cherrywood rocker, rocking slightly. "My sister Trinity just left a little while ago. She's very excited about my new job and we called our youngest sister and told her."

"I hope they're happy about it."

"That's a huge understatement. It's a wonder you didn't hear Trinity screaming for joy."

He chuckled. "I told Caroline. In her own quiet way I think she's pleased."

"I'm sure she didn't say anything."

"No, but I got a little response because she nodded. That's more than I usually get, so I took that as a positive sign. She also gave me a long look and I think that was another affirmation."

"I hope so." She thought about the little girl and grew somber after the evening with Trinity.

"We already miss you being here" he said in a deeper tone of voice that caused another flurry to her heartbeat.

"I'll be back soon enough."

"No, not soon enough. If you wind things up there sooner, give me a call and I'll send someone to get you earlier. If I can do anything to help you move, let me know."

"Thank you. It's just a matter of putting things on hold for the summer."

"Are there really no guys to say goodbye to?"

"There are really no guys," she said, smiling. "I meant what I said about that."

"You've been shut out of life long enough."

"That doesn't go with the job, remember?"

"This is entirely separate from that. If you'd turned me down on my offer, we would still be having this part of the conversation."

"Stop flirting and getting personal," she said, trying to sound good-natured about it, but meaning what she said. "You make it difficult because you're now my boss, so it's a little strange to tell you what to do."

"Then don't." She detected the laughter in his tone. "You know I could send someone to help you with the arrangements you have to make."

"Thanks, but I'll take care of things here myself," she said, amused that he would try to take charge of what she was involved in at home.

"Some weekend soon, I'll fly your sisters here so I can

meet them and they can meet Caroline and see where you live and work."

"They would love that," she said. "We're not much alike. I'll warn you now, Trinity is a little dramatic."

"She didn't get that from her older sister."

"You don't know me well enough to decide whether I'm dramatic or not."

"I think I do. I'm not much like my brothers, either."

They talked easily about their families, and when she glanced at the clock, she was surprised an hour had gone by. "Will, we should end this conversation. Do you realize how late it is? I need to get up early in the morning."

"I'm enjoying the company. It's worth losing some sleep."

"Stop it. I'm saying good-night now. Good night, Will."

"Good night, Ava. I'd rather kiss you than say farewell," he said in a husky voice.

Her heart beat faster. All summer with him; he could derail her dreams even more if she wasn't careful. She inhaled deeply. She had no intention of letting him do that no matter how appealing the man was. Or what he offered her, because he had already promised enough that she could afford to turn him down in the future. Half a million was a fortune beyond her dreams. The wealth would give her independence to do as she pleased about some facets in her life, including Will Delaney.

"Thank you, Will," she said, remembering his dark gaze on her, trying to avoid thinking about his kisses or his sexy voice as he told her goodbye on the phone.

Will Delaney had just opened a whole new world for her.

Smiling, Will shut off his phone. Before he set it down a tune began to play. He answered the call to hear his brother Zach's voice.

"Had a moment and thought I'd check with you. I'm in the L.A. airport, but I won't be coming home. I'm on my way from Australia to Winnipeg. Any luck with tutors for Caroline?"

"Actually, I've hired the teacher who gave me recommendations. I wanted to get to know her better, and then when she was here, Caroline responded to her in a small way."

"If Caroline responded in the least, it's worth a try. Don't blame you."

"Caroline asked Ava if she hurt. Ava is a widow."

"I'll be damned," Zach said. "Caroline hasn't said a word to me since she lost her dad. That's something."

"It's a small thing, but I'm willing to take it. I just have a feeling about this, and with Caroline asking Ava a question— I couldn't let that go."

"Hell, no, you couldn't. That's amazing. A widow. That's nice for Caroline. Our mother isn't grandma material and our stepmother has never been interested in Caroline."

"Zach, Ava isn't exactly grandma material, either. She's twenty-eight. Widowed in college. They married before they graduated. She doesn't date though."

"Okay. I assume she's good-looking."

"Good-looking wouldn't have mattered if I hadn't thought she'd help."

"I know. Well, that's good news. I'll pray for Adam's dear Caroline and this tutor. What's her name?"

"Ava Barton."

"I'll meet her next time I'm home. Whenever that may be. Let me know how things go. When does she start work?"

"Next Monday."

"Good deal. And good job, Will. Hey, they're calling my flight."

"So long, Zach. Take care." Will broke the connection, staring into space, but lost in thought about Ava.

After a busy week, Ava wound everything up by Saturday. She'd taken Trinity for a goodbye dinner, then woke up early and excited on Sunday. She dressed with care, in blue linen slacks and a matching shirt, and wound her hair into a bun, fastening it with a clip. She made some last-minute phone calls, did some research and waited for Will.

Promptly at 3:00 p.m. her doorbell rang.

When she opened the door, her breath caught. Tall and handsome, Will smiled at her and stepped inside, closing the door behind him. His brown eyes swept over her, stirring tingles. The impact of seeing him was greater than ever, and she locked her fingers behind her back.

"Hi. You look gorgeous," he said in a husky voice.

"Thank you. Is it possible for you to keep this a purely business arrangement?" she asked, hating the breathless sound of her voice.

"No," he said, smiling at her, an irresistible smile showing snow-white teeth and creases bracketing his mouth. "I don't think it is for you, either, only you won't admit it. I'll bet your pulse is racing right now because, all business aside, we react to each other." He reached out to place his fingers lightly on her throat to feel her pulse. She twisted away from him.

"You've proven your point," she remarked dryly. "I'm ready." She turned to pick up her things, but he stepped past her to shoulder the carry-on and gather her other bags.

She locked up, and when they stepped out, the chauffeur standing by the limousine came forward quickly to take her luggage.

"I'm glad to get you back to Dallas."

She smiled at him. "So I might as well save my breath on telling you to keep all this impersonal?"

"Now you're catching on. If you didn't react to my flirting and remarks and kisses, I would back off, but you do respond." He leaned down by her ear. "You set me on fire with your responses."

"Stubborn, stubborn," she said before stepping into the limo.

Looking relaxed, Will sat facing her.

"Rosalyn is with Caroline until we get home. Then she is taking tonight off. Tomorrow I'll be home since it's your first day. Did you get everything taken care of to your satisfaction?"

"Yes. With money in the bank, it gets easier."

Will nodded. "Good. I don't want you to have any regrets. Far from it. We'll be home in no time."

In what seemed a short flight to Ava, they landed at Love Field in Dallas. As soon as they were in his mansion, Will turned to her. "I'll have your things put away."

"Thanks, Will. Where is Caroline? I'd like to say hello to her."

"She's probably upstairs with Rosalyn." They headed upstairs, and he knocked lightly on Caroline's door. She sat on the floor playing with dolls and her small brown bear. Rosalyn sat nearby with a book in her hands. Caroline stood up, her gaze on Will although she gave Ava one brief glance.

"How's my girl?" Will asked, picking her up to hug her and kiss her on the cheek. He turned to Ava. "Looks who's here. She'll be staying with us now for the summer."

When Caroline's eyes widened, Ava took it for a hopeful sign. She had uncustomary butterflies in her stomach over trying to help Caroline, yet she was hopeful she could do so even in a tiny degree.

Five

"Hi, Caroline," Ava said, and without waiting for an answer she turned to Rosalyn. "It's nice to see you, Rosalyn. Will, I'll go to my room to freshen up and then I'll go downstairs."

She turned and left, trying to keep things low-key with Caroline. She knew the child would have to come to her, not the other way around.

She unpacked, giving Will time with his niece. After an hour, she went downstairs to look for him. She finally spotted them outside in the sparkling pool.

Declining to join them, she sat near the pool and watched Will with Caroline. Finally he swam a lap and then climbed out.

Ava drew a deep breath as her gaze ran over his muscled body and the thick mat of dark chest hair that tapered in a narrow line to disappear below his black swim trunks. Her mouth went dry and she could not keep from looking at his broad chest, lean body, long legs. He was tanned, fit and handsome. He raked his wavy black hair back from his face, wrapped the towel around his middle and strolled over to pull a chair close to her. "You should have joined us."

"I will some other time. Caroline seems to enjoy herself."

"She loves to swim. It's easy to tell that she likes the water. She always has, and learned to swim early. My brother Adam swam with her all the time."

"You said you were closest to your older brother."

"Yes. I'm getting closer to Zach. There's a big age gap between Ryan and me. We're not as close and we have different interests."

"I'm closer to Trinity, but that's because of age. Now that she's in college, I'm getting closer to Summer. Summer is the one who will be the teacher so we'll probably become even closer later."

All the time Will talked, he kept his attention on Caroline, as did Ava just out of habit from watching kids at school and on playgrounds. One time Caroline went under; when she didn't bob right up, Will was almost in the pool before she popped up, splashing and obviously enjoying herself. While he paused at the edge of the pool to talk to her, she splashed around. She played with a ball, and after a few minutes, Will returned to his chair.

"She does that sometimes. It always scares me. So far, I've never had to pull her out, but she still scares me."

"Better to be safe," Ava said. "How long will she stay in?"

"Probably until I get her out. She loves the water. I told Rosalyn to keep a close eye on her because I always worry about her wandering off and going in without anyone watching. She's getting big enough now it's not the worry it was. When we're not in the pool, we keep the gate locked on the surrounding fence. The gate helps, but I travel, and when I'm away, I don't want to worry about something happening to her."

"I don't blame you," she said. "I can see why your brother appointed you guardian."

"I had the gate put up before I became her guardian, way back before she was toddling around. I couldn't bear to have anything happen to her."

"That's good, Will," she said, thinking it was one more facet of Will Delaney that she had to admire. Her gaze ran over his broad, bare shoulders that had dried. His black hair was still wet.

"I'm going to get her out and start dinner. I'm grilling tonight."

She smiled. "I'll watch her so she can stay longer."

"Okay," he said, walking away while her gaze raked over his wide shoulders, down his long legs briefly before she turned her full attention to Caroline. Pulling her chair closer to the edge of the pool, she sat watching Caroline, who swam to the edge and gazed back solemnly.

"You're a good swimmer," Ava said.

Caroline blinked and swam away and continued playing and splashing. Playing, she looked as happy as any other kid, and it made Ava hurt for her.

Finally Will returned to check on food in an outdoor oven. He walked over to the edge of the pool. "Time, sweetie. Dinner will be ready in a few minutes. Leave on your swimsuit. After you dry, you can pull on a T-shirt and shorts."

Caroline climbed out and in minutes she had on a T-shirt and shorts. Slipping on flip-flops, she picked up the small brown teddy bear.

Will held out his hand. "Come over here while I cook. Ava, want to join us?"

She sat near them, aware of Will talking to Caroline, smiling at her, and Caroline gazing back gravely at him.

Through dinner Will talked about trips Caroline had taken to Disney World, things she had seen and managed to include her even though she never said a word.

"You're a talented man," Ava said. "This is a delicious steak."

"Thanks. I've had a good teacher. It's not Caroline's favorite, so soon we'll have fried chicken, which is what she
prefers. But we're not eating a steady diet of drumsticks," he
said, smiling at Caroline.

When dinner was over they moved to the edge of the pool
while Caroline went back into the water.

"You're good with her all the time," Ava said.

"Maybe. I haven't been able to break through that wall she
keeps around herself."

"Has she ever talked to you?"

"Other than 'thank you' and 'please,' very rarely. And that
was when I first got her. Most of the time it was telling me
she wanted her daddy. That's heartbreaking."

"Yes, it is," Ava agreed, watching Caroline splash in the
shallow end of the pool. "To watch her now, she looks like
any kid having a good time."

"That's why I think swimming may be good for her. It's
exercise and may relieve tension in a kid as much as it does
in an adult. It's a healthy, normal activity."

"You're paying me way too much, you know," Ava said.

His dark gaze shifted to meet hers. "If you can bring her
out of this, it will be worth every penny."

"There are definitely no guarantees."

"I never asked for any," he replied, turning to watch Caroline again.

Later, Ava went to unpack while Will took Caroline to bed.
It was a couple of hours later when she heard a light knock
on her door and she opened it to find Will.

"Caroline's fast asleep and Rosalyn is here. Take a break,
come have a drink with me—we have everything from milk
and cookies to fizzy drinks to wine or cocktails. We can talk
about the coming week."

"For a short time," she said, pushing her door wide and
stepping into the hall with him. They got tall glasses of iced
tea and sat on the veranda. Will pulled a chair close to hers.

"I'll be in Los Angeles this week. You have my cell number. I'll leave you my secretary's number because she knows my schedule. You can always get me on my cell. I'll call during the day and in the evening."

"Fine. I can't imagine needing you, and if it's something with Caroline, Rosalyn will be here."

"Yes, she will. She can be quiet and blend into the background so she doesn't intrude. With the staff here, meals will be prepared so you don't have to worry about anything beyond Caroline. If there are any books you want to get for her, go ahead. Charge them to this card," he said, withdrawing a credit card from his billfold.

She took it, tucking it into a pocket. "Thank you. Right now, I have plenty of my own material I can use."

"After the past week and the coming week of staying here and working with Caroline every day, my guess is that by this weekend, you might enjoy an evening out. How about Saturday night?"

Saturday night out with Will Delaney sounded wonderful, but it meant getting sidetracked from the plans for her future even more. He grew more tempting daily and the risk of an affair was constant. Any affair for her would involve her heart and later, it would mean heartbreak, because Will would end it. Yet how tempting it was to think about Saturday night with him.

"I haven't changed my mind about keeping this job separate from my private life. I'm here to work with Caroline. That's all." The words came out automatically, but it hurt to refuse.

He leaned closer, placing his hands on the chair arms on either side of her, hemming her in. Only inches away, his dark eyes consumed her. It was difficult to get her breath and her pulse raced. "You're scared of life."

"You got your way about this summer. Stop while you're ahead. I've already explained to you, I don't want to get tied up emotionally with someone." She could barely get her breath to talk. "The minute Caroline goes to kindergarten in the fall, I will go back to my plans for my school. Particularly now that I have funds. I'm not getting distracted from my goals. I'm going to achieve what I've always dreamed about. And I'm not having a short affair with you, which is what dinner would lead to. Thank you, but we're not going out to dinner." Her voice was breathless and she was beginning to lose her train of thought and get lost in his dark eyes. He was too close, too appealing, too persistent. "We need to keep this a professional relationship. Treat me the same way you do Rosalyn or Edwina," she added.

"That's not at all the same thing and you know it. I'd be asking this if you hadn't come to work for me. You're scared to live again. One dinner and dancing isn't that big a deal. It's not an affair."

"You know that's not all you're asking for. It's a distraction I don't need," she whispered while he focused on her mouth.

"You're a distraction I do need," he replied, leaning close to cover her mouth with his.

Desire blazed in her. While her pulse roared in her ears, her heart pounded. His arm slipped around her waist then tightened before he lifted her to his lap and settled her against his shoulder. His kisses awakened responses unfelt in years. Heat and need grew vital. His boldness consumed her caution as her resistance crumbled.

The distant moan was her own voice, dim in her ears. He held her tightly while she had her hands against his chest.

When he raised his head slightly, she opened her eyes. Dazed, she wanted to pull him back to kiss her again.

"You're ready for a night out. Go out with me Saturday night—you're not making any kind of commitment beyond joining me for dinner away from here instead of eating the way we usually do."

She slid her arm around his neck. "Yes," she whispered, pulling his head down to kiss him again.

Surprise flared in his dark eyes before he kissed her. Relishing their kisses, she closed her eyes. From head to toe she tingled while heat pooled low in her body and an ache built.

Desire spiraled, burning hotly. Ava ran her hand over his broad shoulder, down over his chest while he caressed her nape. Slipping his hand down her back, he pulled her shirt free from her slacks. His warm hand caressed her bare back. Sitting up, she slid off his lap to return to her chair.

"You agreed to go out Saturday," he reminded her and she nodded. She had gone against her own good judgment and plans. Even so, excitement hummed and she couldn't take back her agreement. Just one Saturday night dinner. A few kisses. Nothing more—she could do that without heartbreak.

"Are you in contact at all with Caroline when you're away?"

"Yes. Since we have Skype, I call her daily. She is as silent as when I talk to her in person, but with Skype we're face-to-face."

"That's good to keep the contact and let her know you're interested."

"For the first time since I became her guardian, I feel better about everything concerning her."

"You're reading too much into the one tiny response I got from her."

"No, that was not tiny. It was monumental. A breakthrough."

"Will, stop setting yourself up for a big disappointment. I hope I can reach her, but that one response is no indication. We'll just take it one day at a time."

He smiled as if she had told him he couldn't be certain the sun would rise tomorrow. Exasperated by his high expectations, she shook her head. "Does your mother see her often?"

"No. My mother packed and left when she divorced my

father. She married again, moved to Chicago where she was originally from and never looked back. We hear from her several times a year, see her about once a year. She's not excited over becoming a grandmother and really has no interest in Caroline, particularly since Adam's death."

"That's too bad. I adored my grandmother—the one I knew. The other one died when I was small and I never really knew her. I can barely remember her."

"My mother doesn't deal well with people who have problems. She is not a patient person. Ironically, she does a lot of volunteer work, but it's in the arts, the symphony, that type of thing. She'll be present for the reading of Dad's will, I'm sure. She'll expect to inherit a large amount and she probably will. When it came to money, he was always generous to her."

"He never married again?"

"No. I don't think he wanted to commit. He was sour on marriage. There were women around, but no more marriages."

"Will your brothers be here when the will is read?"

"Sure. Even Zach will come home. You'll meet them all. They already know about you and that you're going to work with Caroline. Do your sisters know you accepted my offer?"

"Oh, yes. So do my folks. Trinity and I have been together this past week."

"So tell me about Trinity and Summer." While she talked he took her hand, lacing his fingers through hers. He was still, and it would be ridiculous to protest the slight touch, so she talked about her sisters. Words came automatically while most of her attention was on the slight physical contact she had with him. Even though it was almost nothing, she tingled to her toes from it.

Conversation shifted and changed to a variety of topics until the moon was high. Ava stood. "It's definitely time to turn in."

He walked inside with her, talking about the coming week. At her door he slipped his arm around her waist to pull her close. This time she didn't protest, but moved eagerly into his embrace, her arm encircling his neck.

Kisses grew heated, lengthening while he pulled her tightly against him, his hand exploring her back, slipping down over her bottom, up again over her back until she stepped out of his embrace.

"It's later than ever. Good night, Will."

Brushing a kiss on her lips, he smiled. "Until tomorrow."

She closed the door to her suite, moving through the empty room quietly, wondering if she would get to sleep for the few hours left in the night. What had she gotten herself into?

He was quickly becoming irresistible to her.

By the time Ava finished breakfast the next morning, Will had left for his business trip. Ava sat on the playroom floor with Caroline and pulled a box from her tote bag. "I thought maybe you like to play games. I have one I hope you'll like. We can try, and if you don't like playing, we'll stop," Ava said, getting out a deck of cards. "See, they're princess cards and each card has a letter on it. First let's arrange them in the order of the alphabet and you can see the princesses."

Ava began laying out the cards. "There are two identical cards that each have the same letter. Here are two cards with *A* and Princess Ann. Here are two *B* cards with Princess Brianna. Next, Princess Carolyn. And then Princess Dorothy. Now, what card comes next?" she said, spreading out five scrambled cards.

While Caroline sat quietly, Ava remained still, waiting to give Caroline a chance to participate. After five minutes had ticked past, Caroline pulled Princess Eileen and placed it in the row.

"Excellent," Ava said. "I'll do the next. Here's Princess Fiona. We can mix these all up and play a matching game."

She slowly went through the simple rules as they began to play. She had wondered whether Caroline would play or not, but the girl began to respond, her mind quick and her memory good.

From the game they went to books, and Ava read to Caroline, but once again, she let Caroline turn pages and knew that Caroline was reading along with her. They worked on letters and numbers through books and games until almost noon.

"Want to swim before lunch?"

Caroline was always slow to respond if she did at all. She gazed back at Ava with huge brown eyes and nodded her head.

"Great. I'm ready for a swim. Let's put on our suits. Do you know where your swimsuit is?"

Caroline slid off the small chair where she sat and disappeared into the next room. Ava followed to see Caroline reaching into a dresser drawer and taking out a pink swim bottom and purple top.

"Great. Put yours on and then we'll get mine," Ava said.

Soon they were in the pool with Ava splashing and laughing. Caroline never laughed, talked or smiled, yet Ava had the feeling that she enjoyed the water immensely.

Rosalyn materialized for lunch and took Caroline to help her dress before they returned to eat.

The afternoon went as swiftly as the morning. Late in the afternoon, Ava swam again with Caroline. This time Rosalyn showed up and said she would watch Caroline while Ava swam.

Ava did laps, constantly checking on Caroline. She ate dinner with Rosalyn and Caroline in the kitchen alcove and spent a quiet evening getting ready for the next day. It wasn't until after ten that she received a text from Will asking about the day. Shortly after her answer, her cell phone buzzed.

"Hi," Will said in a husky voice. "How's it going?"

"We had a good day. She's a bright little girl."

"So how are you doing in the new situation?"

"She's delightful in her own quiet way and it's a challenge. One I never dreamed I'd have."

"Yeah, amen to that one. Adam and I talked about my being guardian, but I never expected the day would come when I really would be. I'm still at a loss."

"You seem to be doing a lot for her," she said, settling in a comfortable chair and kicking off her shoes.

"I wish I could do more. Ava, I'm sorry, but I won't be able to be home this weekend to take you to dinner. I have a large sale pending and I need to be here part of the weekend, and then early Monday I have to be in Fort Lauderdale for a week, so I'll just have to bypass coming home."

Gone two weeks? "We'll manage."

"Don't sound so cheerful to be rid of me," he teased. "I have opera tickets for the next Saturday night. Some people don't like opera, so if you're one of those, I know the performance will not appeal. If you like opera, attend with me."

"Will, that's the Fourth of July. Caroline should see fireworks."

"She doesn't like them at all. The noise scares her. They have a great display at the country club, but she hated it last year and we left."

"Well, I guess fireworks are out. I doubt if she's changed in one year's time."

"The opera is *The Marriage of Figaro*."

"Now you're twisting my arm, because I do like opera and haven't had a chance to go while I was in school."

"Then it's settled. Saturday we'll go to the opera."

"You get your way most of the time, don't you?"

"When it's important I try to. You'll like this performance. I'll try to make the evening enjoyable, maybe memorable."

"You better stop while you're ahead. We're going out, which is what you wanted."

"I can't recall getting a pretty woman to go out with me being as difficult before."

"I don't imagine you do. I have an agenda to follow and I intend to stick to it, but I will go to the opera. Dinner here at your house before the opera."

"Fine. I'm looking forward to it, and to being home."

She rested her legs under her and sat talking to Will for the next hour before she said she would have to go.

Deciding Will was ruining her peaceful nights, she lay in the dark, remembering his kisses and missing him. She was doing all the things she had intended to avoid, yet it was becoming more difficult each day to resist Will's charm. The barriers she had kept around her heart were melting away faster than she would have thought possible, and in truth, she wasn't altogether sorry to see them go.

She thought of each of his features, the wavy black hair, his thick eyelashes framing lively midnight eyes, his broad shoulders, muscled body and long legs. He was wickedly attractive and sinfully wealthy, a devastating combination. On top of that, he cared deeply about Caroline, going above and beyond his duty to try to help her thrive.

The two weeks he was gone passed quickly, but by Friday, Ava had a subject she wanted to discuss with Will. She felt Caroline became even more distant when Will was not around. It was so slight, she wondered if she was imagining it, yet Caroline became a silent, unresponsive child during the time.

Though he called Ava every night after getting in from dinners and appointments, by the time he tried to get Caroline on Skype, she had already fallen asleep. Ava intended to change that. When he was home, Will gave his time and attention to Caroline, but when he was away, he had little contact with her. Ava felt at this time in Caroline's life, she needed Will's presence more.

She wondered how he'd react to that.

Saturday afternoon Ava swam with Caroline, as she had every day. They played water games and swam for over an hour. Finally Ava climbed out and sat on a chaise longue until she was dry. She watched Caroline continue to swim. At four, Ava let Rosalyn take her place while she went to bathe for the evening. Will had called to say he was running late getting home and she should go ahead and have dinner without him.

She was surprised to find herself disappointed. She ate with Rosalyn and Caroline and then left to dress. Will called once more to say he was turning in the drive and he would spend the time left with Caroline until he had to dress to go to the opera.

As she bathed and dressed, Ava thought about what she would say to him when they were together. She wanted him to make some changes, and she intended to get her way on this one.

She slipped into a dark blue dress with simple lines and a deep V neckline. Her hair was piled on her head with locks falling in the back.

By the time seven o'clock rolled around, she went to tell Caroline good-night. Gazing solemnly at Ava, Caroline held the brown teddy bear. Her dark eyes roamed over Ava, and Ava wondered what ran through Caroline's thoughts. "Your Uncle Will and I are going to the opera. He'll come see you before we go. Later, when we get home, we'll check on you."

The girl just stared her, so Ava smiled, told Rosalyn goodbye and left, going down to the front room to wait for Will. She looked at the leather-bound collection of books on the shelves and wondered whether Will had them for show or actually read them.

"I've looked forward to this all day," he said, sauntering into the room.

Her heart missed a beat when she heard his voice. She

turned, and the impact of the sight of him was even stronger than it had been before. Her pulse raced while she smiled at him. In his dark tux, he looked more handsome than ever—or did he seem that way because she hadn't seen him for a while?

"You look gorgeous," he said. "I missed you the past two weeks and I'm glad to be home. I spent about thirty minutes with Caroline and told her we would spend tomorrow together."

"That's good. I'm sure she likes having you here."

"I don't suppose anything changed with her while I was away?"

"No. There's no change, but she seems happy enough. She likes her books, likes to swim."

"I'm sorry I got delayed and couldn't have dinner with you. I'll make up for that, but there were big storms between here and Florida, and it was best not to take the chance."

"That's fine."

"Don't sound so cheerful that I couldn't get home," he said, and she smiled at him.

Will took her arm and they left to ride in a limousine. Will looked relaxed, confident and appealing.

"Soon now I intend to talk to Caroline about getting a puppy," he said. "I spoke to a veterinarian, and he recommended a bichon frise—a lovable small dog."

"That's great. We had a dog all the years I was growing up. A cat, too."

"We're not getting a cat because I know nothing about them. One animal at a time for now. This is a big deal to bring a dog into the house."

"You don't exactly have a pet-friendly house," she said with amusement. "She's going to love a puppy, I feel sure. Will, while we have a chance, I want to talk to you about something I've noticed during the short time I've been here."

"Sure. What's that?"

"Caroline seems slightly more responsive when you're around. She doesn't talk or smile, but she's less withdrawn. For the coming month, if you can possibly rearrange your schedule, I think you should travel less and try to be home more. A lot more."

While he sat in silence, his dark gaze bore into her. "I'll try if you think it will help."

"I could be wrong, but I've spent over two weeks with her now and she's more remote when you're away."

"No one has ever told me that before."

"It's not a real obvious thing, but that's the way it seems to me. It's worth it for you to make a change and see if that helps to have you around."

"My schedule is really busy right now. I've got important appointments for the next three weeks and my work entails a lot of travel. After we lost Adam, I stayed home a lot that first month. Nothing I did seemed to make any difference so I picked up my life as much as I could and went on with it. I can't just cancel everything scheduled. I'll have to rearrange appointments and flights…but if you think this may help her, I'll do it."

"I know you can do this. You have people who work for you who can cover for you. You're not trying to avoid her, are you?"

Again she got an intense stare. "No. I'll arrange it so I'm in town. Or are you saying I should work at home?"

"Not at all. Just try to be there in the evenings. I think it'll help, even though it may be a gradual thing. This kind of situation probably takes time to heal. I don't know much about it, but I'm giving you my opinion from the last weeks' observation."

"Okay, I'll be there more of the time," he said, still study-ing her. "We'll try that for a while and see how it goes."

"Good," she said, thinking it might be good for Caroline, but it wasn't going to be better for her. Will's presence would be temptation, and the more he was around, the more intense the situation would become. Her pulse raced now and she couldn't get her breath around him. What would it be like to have him around constantly?

"Now if I thought you were asking to get me to be near you," he said in a husky, deep voice, "that would be a different view of this request."

His statement made her hot with embarrassment. To her chagrin, she felt her face flush and wished she could do something to distract him or get out of his view. Instead, he kept watching her, a flicker of amusement in the depths of his eyes.

"Maybe this will be a far more interesting week. I should have thought of this myself. A new dog. Home with you and Caroline each night. Home early if I can manage it."

"You're back to flirting again," she said, looking out the window. The sun was still high. There was no merciful darkness to hide her blush. "Stop teasing me. All I had in mind was Caroline. I can go to my room and leave you two to bond."

"Oh, no. This was your idea, and part of the deal has to be that you stay."

"Sometimes. But part of the time it would be good if just the two of you were together. She needs you, and the more you're together, the more she'll bond with you."

"How about you? The more we're together, will it be the more we will bond?"

"That's entirely different and you know it," she snapped. "Stop your flirting. Get back to some impersonal level. Tell me about this opera. I can't recall seeing a performance of this one," she said, knowing full well she had seen it before, but not recently.

"Ah, it's beautiful. You'll like it," he said, summarizing the story quickly as the limo slowed and stopped. A crowd had gathered, and she wondered if her picture would show up in a magazine with her entering the opera on Will's arm.

The chauffeur held the door. Will climbed out and turned to help her.

While they moved through the crowd into the building, he held her arm lightly, yet with Will it was as disturbing as a caress, far from impersonal. During the performance she struggled to avoid glancing at him. After a time the music overrode her awareness of Will.

During intermission, she was introduced to friends of his. Several women gave her frosty stares, turning their smiles on Will.

"Will," a deep voice called, and Ava turned to see a tall, ruggedly handsome man approaching. A stunning blonde with her arm linked through his walked beside him.

The tall man's thick brown hair had unruly waves with a lock falling on his forehead. He was noticeable in the crowd because of his height plus his hawk nose, high cheekbones and pale gray eyes.

As Will shook hands with him, he turned to her. "Ava, meet my friend and right-hand man, my main advisor, Garrett Cantrell. Garrett, this is Ava Barton."

Her hand was enclosed in a firm grip as he smiled at her with a flash of snowy teeth. His smile softened his rugged features, and she smiled in return.

"Will is given to exaggeration, probably because we're longtime friends who have been together since too far back to recall. Let me introduce Sonya Vicente. Sonya, this is Ava Barton and Will Delaney."

"I'm glad to meet both of you," Ava said as the house lights dimmed.

"I think that's our call," Will said. "Nice to meet you, Sonya. See you, Garrett."

"So Garrett is single?" Ava asked as they walked away.

"Yes. Very available, but not marriage material. He's

almost as leery as I am just because he doesn't want to be tied down. Garrett's ambitious and a workaholic. I think he'd really like to be on his own, but I pay him enough that his salary diminishes the temptation to go into his own business. All that plus our long-standing friendship and family closeness. I can't replace him with anyone as loyal, good, intelligent and fun to be with all rolled into one person."

She glanced back over her shoulder, spotting Garrett's dark hair easily. "You make him sound superhuman."

"Nope. Garrett's human, but exceptional and vital to me. Besides such a close friend."

"You haven't even mentioned the stunning blonde."

Will grinned. "I did notice her. Garrett finds the lookers, but they never last."

"Somehow that's the image I had of you until I met you. As you know, my opinion changed and continues to change."

"Thank goodness," he said as they reached their seats. "Although you're right—I appreciate beautiful women, and I'm out with a ravishing one tonight."

"Thank you, but enough of that. This color hair isn't ravishing."

Surprising her, Will drew her close against his side and leaned down to whisper in her ear.

"Oh, yes it is. We can argue that one later tonight," he said, his breath warm on her ear.

Her heart jumped and beat rapidly. "Your attention should be on the stage."

"It is. Somewhat," he added. "I'd really rather look at you."

"You will see me plenty this summer. Tonight and this moment, shift your attention to the stage. I'm enjoying the performance immensely."

"Good. So am I," he said, settling back, taking her hand and lacing his fingers through hers. "So am I," he repeated, smiling warmly at her.

As the house lights dimmed they became quiet, and while

still aware of Will, she was caught up in the music until it was over.

When the applause finally died, they turned to leave. "That was wonderful. Beautiful voices," she said.

"Let's go have a drink. The evening is still early."

"Hardly early," she replied, amused that he would say so when it was almost midnight. "A drink is fine," she replied, unable to resist accepting.

As usual.

Six

He took her to a private club where they had a window table with a panoramic view of the city lights below. After ordering brandies and talking while they sipped, Will stood and took her hand. "Would you like to dance?"

"Yes," she answered, knowing this was turning into the type of evening she had tried to avoid and should keep from allowing to happen again. As she stepped into his arms, all her caution and guilt disappeared. Will was breathtakingly appealing and she danced with him as if floating on a cloud. An old ballad played softly while Will held her lightly. They danced, legs brushing, her arm on his shoulder, her hand high on his back, the soft wool of his coat beneath her fingers. He was warm, close, his aftershave enticing. His dark gaze was on her as they danced, fanning desire into flames.

She was at a loss for conversation, wanting to dance away, just the two of them, and kiss him, knowing he wanted the same. She barely noticed when he danced to a darkened area, pushed open a door and stepped onto the terrace, taking her in his arms to continue dancing.

A breeze caught strands of her hair, blowing a few against her cheek.

"Beautiful," he whispered and her heart beat rapidly.

"It is beautiful out here," she replied without looking around. She still couldn't tear her gaze from his. Her heart continued to race while they moved slowly in time to the music. Will danced around a corner to a more secluded place on the terrace where there were no other couples.

"Will, the music is fading," she said, her heart drumming. She should stop him, go back, get out of the situation. Instead, all she wanted to do was pull him close and kiss him. As if they had the same thought, he stopped dancing and his arms slipped around her waist, drawing her close against him. When his attention shifted to her mouth, she couldn't get her breath.

Winding her arms around his neck, she tilted her face up as he leaned down. His mouth covered hers, opening her lips to kiss her deeply. His arms tightened. She pressed against him and kissed him in return.

Her pounding pulse drowned out all other sounds and her heart raced while she clung to him, knowing she would never forget this night, never forget knowing him. She wanted so much more than kisses, wanted to caress him and love him.

She might as well be tumbling downward in a spiral she couldn't stop. Yet they were on a terrace with people nearby.

"Let's go home," he whispered with his breath warm on her ear.

"Yes," she replied, sinking deeper into involvement, breaking promises to herself, deciding to worry about it later.

He took her arm and they walked inside to get her purse. The moment the elevator doors closed to leave them secluded and alone, Will drew her into his embrace and kissed her. She returned his kiss, but then stepped away.

"Will, we'll be in public when the doors open and you're rather well-known. I don't recall seeing a picture of you kissing someone in an elevator. I don't want to be the first."

He smiled. "There will not be a photographer waiting, I promise."

"Anyone with a cell phone will do, and can sell the pic."

"I'm not that big in the news. I don't think they could get a dollar."

"We won't argue that point. We're on the ground level," she remarked and stepped off the elevator.

During the drive home, she tried to bank desire and get to impersonal topics. She chatted about Caroline, moving on to everyday events and began to cool, become composed and regain a bit of control over herself. By the time they entered his quiet house, she had overcome the wanton feelings that had run rampant at the club.

"Will," she said, "it's been a great evening. I had the most wonderful time and enjoyed the opera enormously. Thank you for a memorable time."

"I had a great time, too," he said, turning for the stairs.

Relieved that he was willing to call it a night, she walked beside him as they headed to her suite. At her open door, she paused to face him.

He placed his hand over her head on the doorjamb and leaned closer, placing his other hand on her waist. Her pounding heart was loud in her ears while his hand was as hot as a brand.

"Will, it's been a wonderful evening. It ends now," she said, wishing her voice were firm instead of breathless.

"This night can't possibly end now," he whispered, moving closer, his arm tightening on her waist as he walked her backwards into her suite and closed the door.

"Will—" His mouth ended her words and his arm pulled her hard against him as he leaned over her and kissed her deeply.

She intended to stop him, wanted to for the first seconds, but then succumbed to her own desires and his. The battle she waged with herself was lost before it begun, even when it flashed through her mind that she was getting more entangled with him each time they kissed.

Her head spun and heat pooled low in her, desire igniting and burning hotly. All the desire she had felt when she had danced with him returned swiftly. She ran her fingers through his thick hair. His neck was warm. His arousal pressed hard against her.

Clinging to him, she kissed him as passionately as he kissed her. Her other hand pushed his coat off his shoulders and then he wriggled slightly so that his coat tumbled to the floor.

His hand drifted down over the curve of her back, over her bottom to pull her up tightly against him.

Wanting him, she shifted her hips, barely aware of his fingers combing through her hair and pins flying. Locks fell over her back and shoulders and he trailed kisses down to her throat. She twisted free the top buttons of his shirt to run her fingers over his warm skin. His hand lightly slipped along her throat and then he caressed her breast, and she moaned as she clung to him.

"Will, we have to stop."

"You don't want to," he whispered in return, showering kisses on her face and throat. He caressed her nape, sending tingles spiraling from his touch, and then she felt cool air. Will pulled the zipper at the back of her dress, slowly opening it and letting his warm fingers trail over her skin.

She stepped free of his embrace, gulping for air, trying for some semblance of control before she succumbed completely to his loving.

"This wasn't in my plans and it could wreak havoc with all of them. It's good night now, Will," she said, stepping back again to keep distance between them. Her heart pounded.

He stood still, his shirt open, his hair tangled on his forehead and his mouth red from kisses. He was aroused, ready for love. She wanted to step back into his arms, kiss and love him. He was sexy, appealing, almost irresistible except common sense was surfacing. She had already crossed lines and let him destroy barriers she could never put in place again with him.

"You don't really want to say good-night. Our kisses and lovemaking won't wreak havoc with any job, yours or mine. This is something aside from jobs. Stop fighting your feelings. This isn't going to hurt you in any manner."

"I have my year mapped out. Any relationship I have has to have commitment and meaning. An affair could really wreck all that, and I have no intention of arguing about it. Good night, Will. And thanks for a wonderful evening."

She could imagine he debated the next move with himself as he stood immobile.

"Good night, Ava. It's been a wonderful night. Especially the last little bit. I'll see you in the morning at breakfast. I'll dream about you tonight."

"I'll forget I heard that," she snapped and got a mocking smile that brought heat to her cheeks.

He caressed her throat. "Dream about you, want you, toss and turn because of you—"

"You're not helping."

"Just telling you how I feel. Darlin', it's been a great evening and I hate to see it end." He held up his hands before she could speak. "I'll do what you want." Picking up his jacket, he left the room and closed the door behind.

She let out her breath. "I hate to see it end, too," she whispered. Now he was larger-than-life, more handsome, sexier than ever. How was she going to cope with over six feet of irresistible male? She was wanted and in some ways, she loved his attention. Her own reaction to him shocked her daily.

When she was ready for bed, she curled up in the rocker to relive the night, minute by minute and kiss by kiss.

At noon Monday Will stood when his brother came striding across the restaurant where they had agreed to meet. Occasionally, Will thought about Zach's looks, so different from the rest of the family except their grandfather Marcus Delaney. With a mass of dark brown curly hair and vivid blue eyes, Zach had a more narrow face. The only Delaney similarity was his coloring, like their grandfather's, which no one else had inherited. Fortunately, he hadn't inherited their grandfather's fiery temperament. He shook hands with Will.

"I've got two and a half hours before I have to be airborne," Zach said as both men sat.

"You've been in the sun."

"Can hardly avoid it in Baja, California, which is where I went after Winnipeg. What's the latest on Caroline?"

"Nothing since I last talked to you, but I have high hopes because I think Ava has bonded with her. Ava keeps telling me not to read too much into it, but no one else has gotten as much response."

"So how long will she be here?"

"All summer."

"That's a plus for Caroline. What about for you?"

"Hardly. She doesn't want entanglement and I damn sure don't. I'm paying her royally to stay this summer." He eyed his brother. "I wish you had time to stop by and see Caroline."

"I always feel like she's not happy to see me since she lost Adam. Sort of 'why are you here and my daddy isn't'."

"I don't think so. She's just got it all locked inside."

"Well, I want to do what I can. Let me help pay this Ava Barton. If she gets through to Caroline, it'll be worth every penny. Ryan will help, too. I'll talk to him."

"No need. Zach, I can afford to pay her. We all can. From

what Dad told us, we're inheriting more. But thanks. I appreciate both of you being willing to help. Makes me feel good to know I can rely on you in a crunch."

"I probably ought to be the one footing the whole bill. You have full responsibility for Caroline, and Ryan stepped up and agreed to let you name him guardian in case something happens to you. I need to do something."

"Don't worry about it. I'll tell you if I need anything."

"Well, I'd like to meet Ava and thank her. Glad to hear you're not getting too close to her because that could complicate your life and her dealings with Caroline. And glad she doesn't have her eye on you for marriage material. Not that it would do any good, but it could mess up the deal for Caroline."

"She doesn't remotely have her eye on me. She keeps trying to hold me at arm's length most of the time."

Zach paused as he started to sip ice water. "Most of the time?"

"Stop worrying. She's absolutely wrapped up in her plans to open a school, and now she's making enough money to do so. She has no serious interest in me nor do I in her. She is special, though, and I want to get to know her. She's intelligent, gorgeous and ambitious—I find that irresistible."

"I believe you do," Zach said, studying him. "Okay. How's Garrett? Still acting as your right-hand man?"

"Same as ever. One beautiful woman after another with him. Will you be here for the reading of Dad's will?"

"Yep. As soon as we know the date. It'll be good to be together even if it's for an occasion like that."

They paused in their conversation while their hamburgers were delivered and then resumed talking about business, baseball and the coming football season.

With a glance at his watch, Zach stood. "Gotta go. It's time."

Will stood. "I'll head back to the office. Mom called me to

tell me she's coming for the reading of the will. I don't know how she'll act with Caroline. Mom isn't the soul of tact with small children."

"Keep them apart. That'll suit our mother," Zach replied.

"Yep, it will."

"Just another reminder why none of us wants to ever get married. Adam's wife, our mother… Delaney men are not meant to marry," Zach stated. He offered his hand to shake Will's. "See you soon."

"Sure, Zach."

The brothers parted for their cars. Will climbed into his and headed to his office, his thoughts on Ava and the evening.

Will had told Ava he would be in town all week and home by five each day. To her surprise, he arrived at half past four—while she and Caroline were in the pool. Had she complicated her own life by asking him to be home with Caroline more than he had been in the past?

He changed to swim trunks and returned to join them. The minute he swam close, Ava treaded water. "Since you're here, I think I'll turn her over to you so you two can do a little bonding. I'll get dressed and see you over dinner."

"So no hope of talking you into staying with us awhile?" he asked while Caroline splashed at the far end of the pool.

"Not unless you really need me to be here. I would like to get dressed."

"Go ahead. I'm here now," he said, causing her to speculate if he thought she meant she was tired of being with Caroline.

"I think it will be good for her to get your undivided attention for a while. This is a chance for the two of you to have a stronger bond."

"Sure, sure. I'd like to have a stronger bond with you."

"No, you wouldn't really. You aren't interested in any

strong bond, any more than I am. We both have other plans for our futures."

"I didn't mean a marriage bond."

She laughed. "I know you didn't. You've made that clear. I must not have made it clear how I feel."

"Yes, you have, but you're shutting yourself away from excitement and real living."

"And you're willing to provide it all."

"You've made your point. I'll make mine later. Come back out and join us. She'll like having you around."

She smiled at him and swam away to climb out, looking back over her shoulder when she picked up her towel to find him in the same spot, still watching her. She wrapped her towel around her, picked up her T-shirt and headed inside. At the door, she glanced back again to see him playing with Caroline.

Dinner was relaxed, with Caroline saying nothing, yet she was eating better than Ava had seen her eat before. The small brown bear Ava had given her was on a nearby chair.

"Caroline, I want to show you something," Will said. He got up and left the table to return with a folder in his hand. "We thought you might like to have a puppy."

Caroline's eyes opened wide as she gazed at him.

"I brought some pictures of different breeds of dogs. Look at these," Will said, spreading them on the table. "See if you like one in particular."

"Caroline, they're so cute," Ava said, looking at the pictures.

Will told her the various breeds and mixes, pointing to each of six pictures. "Do you see one you like better than the others?"

Caroline sat quietly studying the pictures, picking up first one picture and then another. She turned a picture over and in a moment she turned the second over to place on top of it. Will sat patiently waiting, as quiet as his niece.

"Will, they are adorable puppies," Ava said, looking at two that were so cute she couldn't imagine Caroline wouldn't pick one of them.

Will nodded. "What puppy isn't cute?"

Caroline picked up one picture, studying it intently. She held it out to Will. "I want this one," she said softly.

He flicked a glance at Ava and she could see his joy that Caroline had spoken to him.

"Then I will get you a puppy like that one," he said, putting down the picture, which Caroline picked up and studied. "Caroline, the puppy is a bichon. That's what kind it is and why it looks like it does. The little papillon has that name because *papillon* is French for butterfly, and that puppy has butterfly-shaped ears. Its ears make one think of a butterfly. Tomorrow I will take you and Miss Ava with me and we will get doggie things—we'll need a feeding bowl and some puppy food, some toys for the puppy and a bed. Do you want to go?"

"Yes," she answered.

Will picked her up and hugged her, closing his eyes a moment. Ava glanced away, realizing it was an emotional moment for him.

"All right, sweetie, we'll go tomorrow afternoon. I'll take off about three o'clock and come get both of you and we'll go to a local breeder. We'll have to get a collar and a leash."

He got another faint smile and he hugged her again lightly before setting her down. "We'll get a little crate for the puppy to sleep in and we'll have to find a place in your room to put it. The first few nights it might cry."

She looked up at him while he talked. He took her hand and they walked to the sofa where he sat. She held the picture and turned to run back and get her brown teddy bear before climbing up beside Will.

"You like the idea of a puppy, don't you?"

She nodded her head, looking intently at the picture she held.

"We'll have fun with it. But puppies do have sharp teeth. They bite things because they want to chew. They have baby teeth and like to chew. They don't mean to hurt."

Ava followed them and sat nearby, listening to the conversation and hearing the excitement in Will's voice. Caroline had an eager expression as she sat quietly listening.

"Miss Ava had a dog when she was a little girl, didn't you?" Will said, pulling her into the conversation.

Ava nodded and talked about her dog, and then Will told about the family dog they had when he and Caroline's dad were growing up.

Finally, he stood, picking up Caroline, who still clutched the picture and her bear. "We're off to bed now. Miss Ava has read you stories today, so it's my turn."

Ava stood. "Good night, Caroline." She patted the child's shoulder and impulsively brushed her cheek with a kiss. "We'll play some more games tomorrow and talk about puppies."

As soon as they left the room, she began to clear the table. Edwina would be in to clean in the morning, but Ava saw no reason to leave a mess. She filled the dishwasher and had everything tidy and still no sign of Will. She went to the library and discovered lower shelves that held some children's books. Some were tattered and worn, some the vintage of her own childhood books. Curious, she pulled out one on dinosaurs and opened it to see Will's name printed neatly inside the cover and "six years" written below his name. She smiled looking at the book, imagining Will poring over it as a six-year-old. Ava replaced the book and looked through a couple more. She was surprised the books weren't in Caroline's room.

She heard his footsteps and turned to see him striding toward her. He picked her up and spun around with her.

"Hey!" she exclaimed, laughing as he set her on her feet.

"Did you see the response I got tonight? You caused that, Ava. It's a miracle. She talked to me and I got a little smile from her."

"I'm thrilled and happy for you and for Caroline, but Will, it's just baby steps. It's a tiny, slight progress."

"It's monumental, and you haven't been here that long. Why in hell I never thought of a puppy for her, I don't know except I'm not accustomed to being a dad. There's no school for fatherhood. I didn't even have the usual nine months to adjust to the idea and learn a few things. Thank heavens I decided to fly down and meet you in person," he said, looking at her. Locks of dark hair had fallen on his forehead while excitement sparkled in his eyes. Their gazes met and the moment changed. Her heartbeat quickened and her lips parted. The expression in his brown eyes transformed. Desire became flames in their dark depths and she could barely get her breath.

He lowered his head to kiss her. The moment his mouth covered hers, urgency and need swept her. She moaned softly, lost in wanting him, knowing she was breaking all her own rules for herself, yet unable to resist. She wanted his arms around her and longed for his kisses.

His arms tightened around her, drawing her close against him as he leaned over her to kiss her possessively. Her heart pounded while she slipped her arm around his neck. He held her with one arm while his other hand caressed her nape and then her back, moving to her waist to tug her blouse free of her slacks. His hand slipped beneath the silk to caress her breast as he shifted her slightly. His warm hand on her breast stirred a shower of tingles, sparks that fell on growing fires within her.

She moaned, her voice dim in her ears. She poured herself into her kisses, wanting him blindly, tossing all caution aside, knowing there would be another time to worry about succumbing to him.

"Ahh, Ava, you're marvelous," he whispered, showering kisses on her, and then his mouth settled on hers again, a fierce, passionate kiss that made her ache with desire. He pushed away the flimsy lace bra she wore and cupped her breast. As his thumb lightly circled her nipple, she gasped with pleasure, moving against him.

She tugged his shirt free, slipping her hand beneath it to run her fingers across his muscled chest, tangling her fingers in his thick chest hair, relishing being able to touch him as he caressed her.

A dim voice of caution persisted and she finally stepped back. "Will, this isn't part of why I'm here and it doesn't fit my plans. I don't want a summer fling and I'm not ready for any emotional upheaval." The words tumbled out breathlessly. She moved away to pull her clothes back in place and give them both a chance to cool. Reason and caution should prevail. Yet as she tried to cling to logic, she longed to step back into his embrace and kiss him.

His breath was warm on her nape and he moved close behind her, his arm circling her waist. He pressed against her backside, drawing her against him.

"You're fabulous, and I want to kiss and touch you all night. You need to live again, Ava. You're shutting yourself away. Touching and kissing isn't commitment. Stop being afraid to enjoy life a little."

"I can't get emotionally involved," she repeated, turning to face him. "Are you listening to me?"

He continued to hold her. "Yes, I hear you," he replied, his gaze traveling over her features while he combed long strands of her hair away from her face. He gazed into her eyes again and then leaned close to kiss her.

One more kiss, and then she would make him stop and

mean it. Time and thought ceased and she was consumed by his kisses that grew more passionate. His arm tightened around her waist, holding her tightly against him. She had one arm around his shoulders, one hand on his back.

She pulled away and tried to catch her breath. "Will, let's get back to safe topics and just talk."

"All right, for now." He stood beside a sofa. "Come sit while we talk."

She curled up in one corner of it. He sat facing her a few feet away, but he stretched out his arm across the back to touch her hair and wind his fingers in it. While the slight tugs on her scalp made her tingle, she tried to ignore them.

"So do you know where to get a puppy like the one she picked out?"

"Yes. I've even seen the available litters and all are either ready to pick up this week or will be by next week. The puppies are twelve weeks old now, which is a good age. We'll have to drive to Fort Worth to get the one she selected."

"That's all great, Will."

"The Yorkie litter is in Lubbock. Frankly, I'm glad she didn't pick that one or we would have had a long drive."

"Which you would have done without any protest," she said, amused that he even voiced the complaint about the drive when he was so eager to make Caroline happy.

"Besides, you could meet my parents, since they live in Lubbock." She smiled. "I think Caroline will love having a puppy so much."

He turned strands of Ava's hair in his hand. "I like being at home in the evenings. I've always traveled a lot so this is new for me."

"Good. It'll be better for your niece. That could be why she was more responsive tonight."

"I don't think so. We got more out of her today—that's your doing. And the pup. I've been around all along. Though, granted, not for those two weeks. So how did reading with her go today?" he asked, winding the lock of hair around his finger.

"No different than yesterday. I don't see that as a setback."

"I agree. I had lunch with my brother Zach today. I couldn't bring him home because he was short on time. He'll be back when they read Dad's will. You'll meet all my family then—my mother will be here briefly, both brothers. Garrett, who you met at the opera, will be present because he's like a brother. His dad worked for mine and they were close. The reading shouldn't take long and I expect it will occur soon."

Listening, she looked into his thickly lashed dark eyes and thought about their kisses. The new dog, Will's enthusiasm, his conversation, all of it diminished until she didn't hear anything for thinking about his kisses and how she was getting closer to him, drawing nearer to seduction.

After a while he leaned toward her and held her chin lightly with his fingers. "You haven't heard a word I've been saying."

Jolted, she focused on him. "Yes, I have."

"Right," he stated in a tone that conveyed the opposite. "So what do you think?"

Her face was hot. "Sorry. I was thinking about Caroline's puppy."

"No, you weren't. You were thinking about us."

"There is no 'us.'"

He smiled knowingly. "So tell me, where's this school of yours going to be located? Do you have property yet?"

"I'm looking at areas in Austin and also San Antonio. San Antonio has a diverse population, although there isn't a city in the U.S. that can't use a school focused on reading. It will probably be Austin because I know the city better and it will be easier. I won't have to move."

"What about Dallas?"

"No. Austin is where I live and I'm more familiar with the city."

"Who is looking for property for you?"

She told him the name of the real estate group, aware he had scooted closer and stroked her nape lightly, stirring far more tingles than he had by twisting locks of her hair. He asked questions about her plans, nodding, making few comments and no suggestions, which surprised her. She suspected wheels were turning in his mind and he could make quite a few suggestions if she asked for them.

Several times while they talked about various topics, she intended to tell him it was time to go. Instead, she was pulled into the conversation until she saw it was almost three in the morning. She stood. "Will, it's so late. I'll fall asleep tomorrow while I play with Caroline."

"I doubt that, but we can turn in," he said, standing and draping an arm casually across her shoulders as he walked beside her.

Chatting about the next day's schedule, they headed out of the room. She waited while he locked the front door and then they climbed the steps. Each step brought her closer to telling him good-night and the awareness they would kiss sent her pulse galloping again.

Would she be able to turn him away at her door?

Seven

He entered her suite with her, closed the door and drew her into his arms to kiss her. She held him tightly, kissing him with pent-up passion that was tinged with anger that he had broken through the barrier she had kept around herself for the past six years.

Leaning against the closed door, he pulled her against him while he kissed her. Desire blazed, a stronger need than ever. After a few moments, he shifted slightly and his fingers tugged free the buttons of her blouse. While his hands flew over her, clothing fell away. His warm hands cradling each breast fanned flames. His gaze roamed slowly, carefully over her.

"You're beautiful," he whispered, his dark brown eyes a silent echo of his words. He leaned down to draw his tongue in circles on her nipple, a leisurely torment before he moved to her other breast. Gripping his arms, she gasped with pleasure. Wanting the slight barriers between them gone, she yanked free his shirt. He pulled it over his head to toss aside.

His bronzed chest rippled with muscles, capturing her attention. She had to touch the thick mat of chest hair that narrowed to a single line that disappeared below his belt. The moment her fingers made contact, he groaned, his response stirring her in turn.

"We do things to each other," she whispered.

"Magic," he whispered, then kissed her neck.

He wrapped her in his arms again to hold her close and kiss her. Why did it seem urgent to kiss him? Realizing she was racing headlong toward calamity, she stopped.

She stepped away, yanking up her blouse and holding it in front of her.

"Good night, Will. You have to go."

His dark gaze bore through her while he reached out to grasp her shoulder. "Sometime soon you will not tell me to go." His eyes burned with such intense desire, her knees were weak. He leaned close to brush a kiss on her mouth while he caressed her nape. She gasped and closed her eyes. "See, you respond. You can't keep from it because this is what you want, too, darlin'. It's good between us, but there is so much more."

"What I want is commitment," she said, the words tumbling out.

"I think you've had my commitment since the moment we met."

"Commitment to an affair," she said, gasping for breath.

He showered kisses on her throat and face and then his mouth settled on hers again.

How long they kissed she couldn't guess. Finally, she stepped away. He caught her waist, leaning forward. "Good night, darlin'. I'll dream about you." He brushed a kiss on her lips and then was gone, closing the door behind him.

His shirt lay on the floor. She picked it up and tossed it on a chair. She wasn't going after him and she didn't think he would come back for it.

She touched her lips. She was letting him get too close in too many ways.

Her thoughts churned as she got ready for bed and then lay in the dark to steep in regrets. She had to do better in keeping him at a distance. Avoiding him was impossible. He grew more irresistible each time they were together. How long before seduction? And then how long before heartbreak? Her thoughts shifted to Caroline. Had today really been progress, or just a temporary ripple? Only time would tell. Ava prayed the puppy turned out to be what Caroline expected and hoped for. Ava knew of many programs that brought together animals and children for therapeutic purposes. Hopefully, a puppy would be something Caroline could love and respond to. Another question that only time could answer.

The next day it took no time to realize Caroline was excited about the puppy. She picked out books about dogs to read and once she gave Ava a smile. Ava's heart turned over and she realized she was grasping at tiny responses as much as Will did.

She noticed Caroline was looking often at the tall nursery-rhyme-character clock in her playroom and she realized for the first time that Caroline could tell time.

She wrote Will a text that Caroline was watching the clock and thought she was excited and anxious for him to come home to take her to pick out her puppy's things. Ava hesitated before sending the message, unsure if she should get Will's hopes up, but a minute after she sent it, she received a brief reply that he would try to come home early.

When Will arrived home at three, Caroline was ready, holding the brown bear and waiting quietly.

He came striding into the room in his charcoal suit. Handsome, oozing vitality, Will had a dynamic presence that charged the air with electricity. He flashed a wide smile at Ava and picked up Caroline to hug her. "Ready to get your puppy a crate and bed and toys?"

Caroline nodded. "Yes, sir. And a collar."

"We'll get a collar, too. Shall we go?"

In the pet store, Ava enjoyed watching the two of them walking around while Will talked to Caroline about her choices. She pointed at what she wanted, and Will would put it in a basket he carried. When she selected a collar, she smiled briefly at Will. She placed the collar in the basket he carried and when she turned away, he gave Ava a glance that indicated how thrilled he was over Caroline's response.

When they returned home, they picked a place in the kitchen for the dog dishes, and upstairs a perfect spot in Caroline's playroom for the puppy's crate. Caroline set out the toys while Will put away the puppy food.

Finally, it was bedtime for the tired little girl. Will carried Caroline to bed. While he was gone, Ava left him a note that she was going to turn in early. She hurried to her suite to close the door on another night of temptation. It would be more fun to spend the next few hours with Will, but better if she didn't. All the time at the pet shop her pulse had galloped. She was drawn to Will more each day, yet she hadn't changed her feelings about an affair. Will was utterly opposed to marriage and serious commitment—the things she cherished most. The safest thing to do was to keep her distance when she could.

By ten o'clock, she was more restless than ever and wished she hadn't been so hasty in shutting herself away from him.

She didn't fall asleep until nearly morning, and then it was fitful and filled with dreams that involved Will.

The next day was another like the previous one with Caroline watching the clock and being far more wiggly than normal. In the early afternoon after lunch, Ava read a book Caroline had selected. When she finished, she picked up another one.

"Did you like your dog?" Caroline asked.

Startled by Caroline speaking to her, Ava tried to avoid showing her surprise. "Yes, I did. We had a Labrador retriever, Gus. We loved him and he loved us."

Caroline nodded.

Ava was so pleased that Caroline had asked her a question. It was a very good sign.

Will wanted Ava to go along to get the pup, so once again the three of them climbed into the limo, a travel crate, leash and a toy at the ready.

Ava took a camcorder, wondering whether Will ever took pictures of Caroline.

They drove to a tall two-story house in a north suburban area of Fort Worth. A friendly woman introduced herself and showed them in, taking them to the garage where a mother dog was sprawled on a blanket. Caroline's eyes were wide as she watched fluffy puppies wandering around her.

"Now, Caroline, you pick out which one of the puppies you would like to take home," Will said.

Two puppies wandered to Caroline; one chewed on her shoe. Will leaned down to pick up the puppy and hold it so Caroline could see its face. He reached out and scooped up another. Ava watched the two of them and she prayed the puppy would make a difference in Caroline's life.

After deliberating and looking at each puppy several times, Caroline finally picked one up and held it carefully with Will's help.

"This one," she said to him.

He shot a glance at Ava and she smiled, her heart leaping because of the moment that was significant for them.

"You want that puppy? You're sure?"

"Yes, please," Caroline answered, nodding her head.

Will settled up with Mrs. Winston, the breeder, then carried the puppy to the car and placed it in the crate. Caroline sat beside it, her arm on the crate while she watched the puppy, Will talking warmly about the dog.

By they time they got home and had the pup and its belongings unloaded, Ava left Will and Caroline while she went to her room to freshen up. After a while, she walked back to the playroom to see what was happening.

Will lay on the floor with his shoes kicked off. His shirt was pulled out of his slacks and his tie was gone, the shirt's top buttons unfastened. He was stretched out, playing with the pup while Caroline sat facing him, holding a toy sock monkey for the dog. Ava's heart missed a beat at the sight of Will and his niece. He was laughing, playing with the dog and talking to Caroline, who laughed at the pup's antics.

In that moment Ava had to face the fact that she was falling in love with Will. Sadness for the loss of Ethan no longer was a solid wall around her, enclosing her feelings and her heart.

She stepped inside, going to sit near them.

"Come join us," Will said. "This is a great pup. We're going to have to give it a name so it will come when we call it. And it's a girl, so it has to be a girl name. I've been waiting for you to come to help think up a name."

"She looks like a snowball," Ava said. "Snowball? Powder? Puff? My dog was Gus. Gussie for a girl."

"I thought of Millie, Tiny, Princess. That's seven names to choose from. Miss Ava, what do you like best?"

He ignored Caroline, an uncustomary occurrence when she was involved. Ava wondered if he was trying to avoid pinning down Caroline when she wouldn't respond. Or if he had another reason.

"I prefer my names. Maybe Powder."

"Too much like a cat name," Will stated. "So is Puff and so is Snowball."

"No, it's not," she argued lightly, thinking he looked more appealing than ever, stretched on the floor, playing with the dog and concerned with Caroline.

"Muffy," Caroline said.

As if it were the most normal thing for her to suggest a name, Will repeated it, "Muffy. That's a good name. All right, Caroline. Muffy it is. Muffy is your puppy and if you want to name her Muffy, we will."

"I think that's a cute name," Ava agreed, sitting in a chair, wanting to intrude as little as possible on uncle, niece and puppy.

"We'll call her Muffy, and in a day or two, she'll know her name. I have a trainer coming by who will work with her every day. He'll be here tomorrow and work with her for a week, then come back when she's a little older because she's too young now for a lot of the training."

Caroline picked up the pup to place it in her lap. The white pup stretched out, falling asleep in minutes. "She's a baby, Caroline," Will explained. "She's worn out and she'll sleep soundly for a little while because that's what most babies do. When she wakes up she should go outside—I'll take her— and then she might want some water."

Later, when dinner was finished, Caroline slid out of her chair and ran to sit with Muffy.

"You've handled this just right, Will," Ava said.

"I never been so at a loss as I am with her," he said quietly while Caroline ran around and Muffy chased her. Laughing, Caroline climbed in a chair.

"Look at her laugh, Ava. She hasn't done that since we lost Adam."

Ava sat back, observing the scene, watching Caroline reach down to pet Muffy.

When it was story time, Ava got up to go, crossing to Caroline to touch her head lightly. "I'm glad you have Muffy. Dogs are fun and they become part of the family. Good night," she said, brushing Caroline's cheek with a kiss.

"Good night, Miss Ava," Caroline said quietly.

Ava smiled at Caroline. "Good night to Muffy, too," she said, touching the pup's head as it slept again in Caroline's lap.

As Ava walked out of the room, Will came after her. "Ava, wait."

She turned. He had changed clothes after dinner, pulling on jeans and a T-shirt. He caught up with her. "Wait for me downstairs. I missed you last night."

She could refuse. Instead she nodded and he headed back to Caroline.

She went by her room to take the clips out of her hair and let it fall loosely around her shoulders. With a cursory glance at herself, she went downstairs to wait, taking her cell phone to send texts to her sisters.

It was over an hour before Will came through the door. Closing the door behind him, he crossed the room in long strides just as he had before to pull her up into his arms and hug her. He leaned away. "Thank you! You have to admit today was a big, giant change."

She smiled at him. "I will agree it was. You're a good dad, Will. You handled everything well."

"I'm flying by the seat of my pants with her. I don't know what's best, but she talked to us. She named the pup and said she wanted it. She's even laughed out loud twice. Ava, I can't tell you how grateful I am."

"I still say I haven't done that much, and you would have thought of a puppy before long yourself."

"I might not have. I haven't in all the time Caroline has been in my care."

"It's a beginning, Will. Maybe she will be happy enough to talk more often." Ava turned to walk away to sit. Will caught her arm, turning her back to face him.

"Ava, come here," he said in a husky voice, wrapping his arms around her and kissing her. His kisses were passionate, driven, and she was swept away, unable to resist kissing him in return. She was adding to her problems with him. Night by night, she was binding her heart to Will in a manner that was going to hurt when she broke away.

"I want you," he whispered.

"Will, don't mistake your gratitude for something else. There can't ever be anything much between us."

"Oh, yes, there can," he said. "There can be so much. I'm grateful, but I know the difference. You're a gorgeous, sexy woman and we have an electricity we both feel always."

Her heart pounded with his words, magic words that were another tie that bound her. He framed her face with his hands and kissed her possessively, his kiss conveying his intent. She resisted for seconds and then kissed him in return, wrapping her arms around his slender waist, holding him tightly while they kissed.

His hands roamed over her, caressing her, unfastening buttons. She should stop him, but it was impossible. Too soon she would be gone, back into her busy working life and her solitary hours on her own.

In minutes he had stripped his shirt and boots, He cupped her breast to caress her while he continued kissing her and then leaned down to kiss each breast while his hands slipped lower, unfastening her slacks and letting them fall.

He stepped back, holding her hips while he looked at her. "You're beautiful," he whispered. He picked her up, carrying her to the sofa where he placed her on his lap, kissing her without pause as his hands moved over her.

When he shifted to lie down, holding her close, she slipped away and stood, turning to gather her clothes. "Will, we're going further and further and I don't want this. I've told you why. We have to work together all summer. I can't get deeply involved with you and I can't have a quick, meaningless fling." She yanked on her shirt and turned to face him. He had walked over to her and slipped his arms around her waist.

"I want you, Ava. You want me, too. You're fighting something that you also desire."

"I'm going to keep fighting you on this. I will not get emotionally involved or too physically involved. I just can't do it. I shouldn't kiss you. I need a solid commitment—you can't give me that."

"Ava, take life as it comes. I'm not looking for a one-night fling. I promise you that. Frankly, I think you're lecturing yourself. This is something you want. We both want. I still say it's time you come back into the world and live a full life the way you were meant to. You're too much a desirable, beautiful woman to shut yourself away and live a solitary, empty life."

"I don't see a summer fling as any solution."

He kissed her cheek, her temple and then her mouth, holding her close. She only had on her blouse and a narrow strip of lace panties. The kiss deepened, changed and became passionate. She was sliding right back to where she had been only minutes ago. She wriggled away from him.

"I'm going, Will. You're too damned appealing, but I do have a shred of willpower."

He smiled faintly at her as he if knew it was only a matter of time until he seduced her. She stepped into her slacks, buttoned them and walked toward the door.

"Ava," he said in a commanding tone that stopped her and she looked back at him. "It's early. Let's sit and talk. This has been a very special day and it's too early to end it now. I want to savor the moments."

She took a deep breath and nodded, caving the minute he asked.

"I agree that it has been a special day. One I think she'll always remember. I hope Muffy works out to be a great pet."

"I'm going to try to see to that. The guy who is coming to train Muffy works on our family ranch. He's excellent with animals. He's trained dogs for us, and horses." While Will talked, he walked over to pick up his shirt and pull it on. Muscles in his smooth back rippled, and she inhaled deeply.

She sat in the closest chair, wanting to avoid the sofa where he could pull her into his arms easily.

In spite of her declaration, she was on fire with wanting him. She had fallen in love with him and she ached to walk back into his arms, kiss him and make love.

She had sense enough to know that was the way to disaster. To get tied up with Will invited catastrophe for her heart, calamity for her school plans. Any woman he saw on a regular basis would be on his terms. And those terms would not include marriage. Eventually, he would be through and walk out of her life, another heartbreak. Ava never wanted that to happen.

She tingled and hoped she could keep from showing how much she wanted him.

He faced her. "Would you like something to drink?"

"Actually, iced tea sounds delicious." She stood to follow him into the kitchen. "Can I help?"

"No. Just sit and talk to me. I feel like shouting for joy. Caroline laughed and talked tonight. It's been a year, Ava. I knew you would be so good for her."

"I can't take credit."

"You should. It's wonderful. I don't think she'll go back to the way she was. At least, I don't think she will as long as she doesn't suffer some other kind of loss."

Ava watched him fix drinks and then they moved to the living area adjoining the kitchen. She took a chair again and he sat facing her.

"I don't hear the puppy, which surprises me."

"These walls are thick, and Rosalyn has the puppy with her. Later, I'll get it and put it in my room where I can keep up with it tonight."

"Another surprise," she stated, smiling at him. "I would

never have guessed you would give up your peaceful sleep to babysit a new puppy."

"One, the trainer isn't here yet. Buck will care for her tomorrow night. Two, I don't want Caroline to hear her crying and worry about her."

Ava smiled.

"I feel so good, as if a huge stone has been lifted off my shoulders. Let's go out and celebrate Saturday night. Early evening. I'll get you back when you want."

"All three of us?"

"No. I don't want to take Caroline out yet. This is too tenuous a thread for me to risk having her retreat back into her shell. She'll be more relaxed at home. Will you go with me Saturday?"

"You are a persistent devil," she teased. With a crooked smile he winked at her.

They sat and talked until two, when she said she had to get to bed. Will walked her to her room and kissed her goodnight with one long kiss.

"Are you still going to get Muffy?"

"Yes. Rosalyn reads until all hours. She'll still be awake. I don't hear any howls or crying. Rosalyn is probably holding Muffy. I think she likes Muffy as much as Caroline does."

"It's been a good day, Will."

"Thanks to you," he said, brushing her lips lightly with his before he left to get the dog.

The next morning after breakfast, Ava, Will and Caroline went out on the lawn to see the trainer playing with Muffy, who was on a leash.

"Both of them seem to be having a fun time," Ava said.

"They are. This afternoon, Caroline, you'll have Muffy with you part of the time and again tonight. This is just for a short time while he gets her trained."

The trainer picked up the dog and came over.

"Ava, this is Buck Yarby. Buck, this is Ava Barton and here is Caroline."

"Glad to meet you both. Caroline, you have a good little dog here. She's going to be a lot of fun for you. I'll show you what she can do after I get her trained."

They talked a few minutes while Caroline petted Muffy, and then they headed back inside to start their day—already off to a very good start.

Will arrived home early from work. He entered the room with the same commanding presence as always, plus this time he carried the puppy. He scooped up Caroline with one arm.

"Hello, hello," he said. "Want to play with your dog?"

"Yes, please," Caroline answered, smiling at him.

"Ah, that's a wonderful smile, sweetie. You have fun with Muffy." He set Caroline down and carefully handed her the puppy. "Hold her gently and be very careful to not drop her because that would hurt her."

"I won't," Caroline said, holding the dog and sitting on the floor to put Muffy in her lap.

Will looked at Ava. "This is good."

"It's been an unusually fine day. Caroline read to me," Ava said, wondering whether her pulse raced over Will's appearance or over being able to tell him the exciting news.

"Wonderful! Caroline, that's fantastic," he said. "Look at Muffy, she likes to have you scratch her ears." Caroline smiled again.

Will tossed off his navy suit jacket and kicked off his shoes, sitting on the floor with Caroline while Ava began to gather books and games to be put away. She listened to Will talk to Caroline a little, and then he sat in silence while they played with Muffy. Caroline laughed when Muffy caught her shoe and tugged on it.

Will picked up the puppy to get Caroline's shoe away from

the dog. He grabbed a dog toy, squeaked it and gave it a toss. Caroline laughed when Muffy dashed after it.

Thrilled by the change in Caroline, Ava sat in a rocker and watched, remaining quiet.

"Muffy, here Muffy," Caroline called. The pup ignored her, and Will stretched out his arm to catch the dog and hand it to Caroline.

They played with the puppy for a long time, and Ava was not alone with Will until that night after he came back from tucking Caroline into bed.

He found her sitting out on the veranda. "Tell me about the day. I've been wanting to hear since I arrived home and you indicated it had been very good."

"I think so. The walls seem to be crumbling for her. When I read today, she started reading when I paused and then I gave her a chance. I'll ask her tomorrow if she'll read for you, and we'll see what she says. She's a good little reader. By the end of summer, Will, she will be more than ready for kindergarten. She should be confident enough to do well."

"Ava, this is just amazing when I think of all I've gone through. You have come in here and quickly healed the terrible hurt that's kept her wrapped up in herself."

"I don't think I can take that kind of credit," she said, aware he sat only a few feet away. He rested a hand on hers, their fingers linked together. He acted unaware of the touch. For her, it was a smoldering flame she could not ignore. It was tangible, a steady contact that made her want more.

"I think Caroline may have been ready," she continued. "I think the puppy has been a trigger for release. She is so happy and excited over Muffy."

"She laughed. She talked to me. She read for you. We'll go out to dinner Saturday night, but I don't think we should leave until near her bedtime. I don't want to skip out on her when all this is happening."

"Very good idea, Will. We don't need to go at all."

"Yes, we do. I want to celebrate and do this as a thank-you."

Her heart skipped a beat. Saturday night. Dangerous for her heart, yet exciting and too big a temptation to turn him down.

Excitement coursed through Will's veins on Saturday. He wanted to be alone with Ava, to take her out where he could hold her, dance with her. Gradually, their kisses were heating and she was letting down her barriers. He wanted to be with her all the time now. He had never wanted a woman the way he did Ava. She was in his thoughts constantly. She wanted commitment—could he make some kind of commitment? Since when had he ever given a thought to commitment? With Ava, the idea seemed different than it had before. He wanted her in his life.

He wanted to treat her to an evening out as a special thank-you for how she'd helped Caroline. Will's throat tightened and emotions gripped him when he thought about the change in his niece.

Ava had been all he had hoped for and more. The break-through had come sooner than he had expected. She was fabulous with the little girl. Ava was just the person Caroline had needed: not too gushy, not too remote. Lost in thoughts about Ava, he dressed in his navy suit, finished combing his hair and left to wait in the downstairs study.

He heard a faint rustle and the click of high heels on the polished wood floor. He turned and his breath was gone as if he had received a punch in his middle. He couldn't keep from staring as he walked toward her.

"Ah, you look stunning," he said, crossing the room to her while his gaze went over her sleeveless red dress with a low V-neck and short skirt. Its plain lines hugged her tiny waist. Her hair was looped and pinned on her head with a few loose strands. Desire burned, hot, intense. He wanted to carry her to bed instead of taking her out for the evening, but that was impossible.

"Thank you," she replied with a smile.

"I won't be able to see anything or anyone tonight except you. You're a very special woman." How could he hold her past summer? He wasn't going to want to let her go. The idea surprised him, but he was as certain as he could be. He wanted her in his life and the thought of her walking out and saying goodbye was unacceptable. When had he developed such strong feelings for her? When had he ever known a woman as special?

"Shall we go tell Caroline good-night?" she asked, breaking into his thoughts.

"Yes. I thought about doing it before I came down, but I wanted to wait until you were ready." He wanted to do everything with Ava by his side.

Together they walked upstairs to the playroom. Before they reached the open door, Will stopped her when they heard Caroline's laughter. His insides squeezed and his throat knotted. Joy and relief rocked him and he tried to control his reaction.

"Listen," he said. "I thought I'd never hear that again." He squeezed his eyes shut. "She's laughing," he repeated, thinking her childish laughter was the most wonderful sound in the world.

He looked at Ava with a burst of gratitude. "I was right about you," he whispered. "You've transformed our lives by finding the way to reach her." He stared at Ava, certain he had never known a woman he cared as much about. Beautiful, breathtaking and she was so much more. For the first time in his life, he was thinking about a serious, long-term relationship.

He took Ava's arm to enter the playroom. Rosalyn sat in a chair while Caroline ran around the room chasing Muffy, who had a toy in her mouth.

"Uncle Will, look at Muffy," she cried and laughed again. "Catch her."

He didn't trust his voice for a moment as emotions tore at him. His eyes burned and he was overwhelmed again.

"She loves for you to chase her," Ava said, filling in for him when he didn't speak.

He pulled himself together. "Want me to catch her?"

"Yes, please," Caroline answered.

"She's been having a very good time with the dog," Rosalyn said, smiling broadly at him.

Will reached out to grab Muffy's toy, catching a leg of the sock monkey. Muffy gave a playful growl and pulled, shaking her head and yanking the toy away from Will. When she dropped the monkey, Will snatched it up to hand it to Caroline. "Throw it for her, Caroline. She'll run and get it."

Caroline threw the sock monkey, squealing with delight when Muffy ran after it.

They stayed longer than he had intended, but he couldn't bear to leave when he saw Caroline laughing and having fun.

Finally, Muffy stretched out on the floor, and Caroline sat down beside her to pet her.

"She's worn out now," Will said, picking up Caroline. "We will tell you goodbye, but we'll be home later. I'm taking Miss Ava to dinner."

He kissed Caroline's cheek and she hugged him tightly.

"I love you," she whispered.

He felt as if he had received another blow. His knees felt weak and he held her close, again having to get a grip on his feelings. "I love you, sweetie, more than anything," he whispered. He leaned away to smile at her, hoping she didn't notice his eyes were teary.

He turned to Ava, who stepped close. "Good night, Caroline. We'll be back after a while."

She brushed a kiss on Caroline's cheek and Caroline reached out to hug her. Ava took her from Will and hugged her lightly. Will drew a deep breath, realizing he might not ever want to let Ava go out of his life. She was rare, special. He watched her set Caroline down. "Good night. Rosalyn, have a nice evening."

Finally Will took Ava's arm and they left. Instead of leaving the house, he led her to the library and closed the door. He turned to face her and she looked at him questioningly.

What was going on?

Eight

"Why are we in the library?" she asked.

As he crossed the room to stand closer, Ava's curiosity grew.

"I have to tell you," he said. "When I picked Caroline up tonight, for the first time since Adam's accident, she told me she loved me."

"Oh, Will!" Ava exclaimed. "I'm so glad. I didn't hear her. How wonderful."

"It is. So is her laughter and her joy in that goofy little puppy that isn't even house-trained yet. And now to have her tell me she loves me. It was monumental. I'm taking you out tonight to thank you. And I have something for you. It's a gesture of thanks for what you've done."

"I think what you're paying me covers that, Will. You don't need to buy a present for me," she said, moved and amused. "Really, Will. You're paying me a fortune."

He pulled a small gift box from his suit pocket and handed it to her.

Surprised, she looked at it and then at him as she accepted it. "This is so unnecessary. I'm thrilled, too, over Caroline. It was heartbreaking to see her shut away in a world of silence." Ava tore away the gold paper and ribbon.

"I intended it as a thank-you for the little responses we've had. Now it's become a gesture for an even bigger thank-you for tonight and how much she has opened up," he said, his voice growing husky with emotion.

She opened a long black velvet box and gasped at the necklace it contained. Set in gold, every other stone was either a sparkling diamond or a brilliant emerald. Shocked, she looked up at him. "Will, I can't take this. It's worth a fortune."

"That doesn't even begin to express my gratitude." He lifted it out of the box. "Turn around."

He placed it on her, fastening it behind her neck.

She crossed the room to the mirror. "I can't imagine wearing this anywhere. I need a bodyguard with it."

He smiled. "I'll be your bodyguard." He walked up to place his hands on her shoulders. "It's a token thank-you. You've worked a miracle."

"Oh, please. I think little Muffy worked the miracle."

"Which was your idea. No, the necklace is a thank-you which you definitely deserve. I want you to have it, Ava," he said in a husky voice. "You mean more to me than any woman I've ever known."

His words thrilled her. Was it just part of his seductive ways? Or did he sincerely mean what he said?

Will glanced at his watch. "Now we should go. We're a little late on our schedule. Since the helicopter belongs to me, it will still be waiting."

"Thank you. I just can't believe this. I keep wanting to look at it," she said, glancing once more in the mirror.

He took her arm and they left. In thirty minutes they were airborne, heading south.

It was after nine by the time they landed in on the helicopter pad on his yacht in the Gulf. Deck lights glittered and she heard a band playing.

"You hired a band?"

"I wanted this to be special for you. Since we're running late and have to get back tonight, I'll give you the tour after dinner."

"Fine." She was still intensely aware of the elegant necklace she wore. So far they had seen only people who worked for him, which suited her because she couldn't get accustomed to wearing something so valuable.

They took an elevator to an upper deck where they crossed to a single table set with white linen. Deck lights and torches burned, giving a soft glow in places, dark shadows in others away from the lights. She wondered how long the band had been playing, but knew they had fair warning when Will would arrive because of the chopper.

"Will, this is beautiful. It's not as hot out here as it is in the city."

"What's really beautiful is the woman I'm with. And exciting."

After they had been seated with wine ordered and poured, Will raised his glass.

"To your success, with all my gratitude," Will said, holding his glass in a toast.

With a faint clink she touched his glass with hers. "I'll drink to my success. I want my school to be all that I hope and have dreamed about."

"You're the right person for it." He stood and held out his hand. "Would you like to dance?"

"Of course," she said, taking his hand. She went into his arms, feeling his warmth, dancing with him. "You lead a charmed life, Will Delaney," she said.

"Sometimes. There's the money and the businesses, which I like. But there's the other side that hasn't been charmed. My mother walked out when I was fourteen, and my brothers and I were shuffled around at schools for a couple of years. I've lost a brother, and then this latest with my father's death and Caroline, which was a tragedy of giant proportions. So all has not been charmed."

"No, I guess it hasn't. That's true for everyone, I suppose."

"No sad faces or gloomy thoughts on this night, though. This is a celebration. I feel like dancing on the table and shouting from the rooftop. I'm so happy about Caroline. There's no way to tell you."

"I'm happy, too, and glad for both of you. She seemed happy tonight. Take very good care of that little dog."

"Actually, I've thought about getting her another one so she has two. That way if something happened to one, we would have the other. Besides, the dogs would be fun for her and company for each other."

"Ask her and see what she would like."

"That I'll do. Is there any way I can help you with your school plans? I have a lot of available resources."

"I'm doing quite well so far, and with the salary you're paying me, I can afford to go ahead with my plans without worrying about grants. Thank you for the offer."

"Enough about business, too," he said. "This is great. I'm glad to have you here. I wish we could take the weekend and sail south, but we need to get back. I want to stay near Caroline right now."

"I agree. I think you need to."

"You, too. You're part of this at the moment. I saw how she hugged you tonight. She doesn't do that with others."

"I was deeply touched."

"Some other weekend before the summer is over, we'll return and take a few days. I can show you some spectacular waters."

"Frankly, your pool in Dallas is beautiful and more than adequate."

"I don't have a band and dance floor at my house—actually, I can have one if I want, but I haven't ever done so. Now for a sexy, breathtaking woman, I might rustle one up at home, but I like it out here on the water. I'd like to show you some sights."

"I doubt if that will happen."

"You can't foresee the future, and I think you would have a grand time."

"I'm sure I would have a grand time," she remarked dryly. "That's part of the problem. I don't want anything to distract me from my plans for my future. It's so easy to get sidetracked and have moments slip away and opportunities lost," she said, thinking about her dad, who had been offered a wonderful sum to sell his Lubbock store and turned it down just before a national chain store opened near him and his business fell off, never to build back up to what it was. She remembered the job offer Ethan had had, their decision to stay and finish school instead. If he had taken the offer, he might not have had the accident.

"I'm not robbing you of your opportunities," Will said, bringing her back to the moment.

"No, because I'm not going to let you," she replied, more for herself than him. Then forgetting her declarations, she became silent, relishing the dance and being held in his arms while they moved around the open deck. Breezes tugged playfully at locks of her hair. The music was great. She would remember this night forever.

There couldn't be many nights in her life like this one. She focused on him, gazing up into his eyes while they danced. The electric current between them escalated. A night to always remember, a man she had fallen in love with even though she didn't want him to know it. Burning desire—the night, the man—all made her want to take what she could and then lock away the memories.

The notion startled her, teased and tormented. The excitement, the exotic night on a yacht, the diamonds and emeralds—Will himself—everything was causing a turnaround in her life. She had been determined to guard against such temptation, yet now she couldn't keep from considering it. The temptation expanded, grew strong. She weighed that against looking back with regrets.

Intending to avoid further complication in her life, she tried to bank desire and curb the wild thoughts. Enjoying the dance, she focused on Will, thinking he had to be the most handsome man she had ever known.

"You're quiet. Nickel for your thoughts."

"You've raised the proverbial penny," she said, smiling. "I'm thinking what a great night this is and how fun it is to dance with you."

"Ah-ha, at least I'm in there somewhere."

"Of course. How could I overlook you? My dashing employer."

"Dashing—I haven't ever been called that. My grandfather might have been. I still need to work on my image."

"Dashing is good. Dashing is exciting."

"In the eighteenth century it was," he said, teasing her.

"Still is in my books."

"I would definitely prefer to hear sexy...."

"I'm sure you would, but we're not going there. Besides, if I told you that, it would go to your head."

"Not so, I think it would go somewhere else instantly," he replied with amusement.

The piece ended and the band launched into a fast number. Will began to dance and she danced with him, moving around him, enjoying the physical release as much as she liked watching him.

He was way beyond a description like *dashing*. He was sexy, hot, virile. What fun he was. But how many hearts had he broken? She suspected a fair number, and she was skirting close to allowing herself to become one more on his list.

When the music ended he smiled at her. "Ready to sit and cool down or do you want to keep dancing?"

"We'll sit and cool for a short time. Actually, I could dance all night if I had a chance, because I haven't in such a long, long time and I love to dance."

"That is an incredible shame," he said, taking her arm to steer her toward their table.

As soon as they were seated, the waiter appeared with salads.

"Will, this is really special and so very nice of you."

"I told you, I'm grateful. Ava, you can't wear that necklace every day...."

She laughed. "I certainly can't. I will rarely wear it. It's too beautiful to take out of the house and too fancy to wear except for special occasions. Very rare in my busy life. A teacher with diamonds and emeralds—not likely."

"Not impossible. But I want you to have something simpler that you can enjoy every day." He produced another box and handed it to her.

Startled, her eyes widened. "Will, this is too much! You can't give me something else."

"I can and I am. Take it. I want you to have it. It's another token of my appreciation. Go ahead and open your present."

She stared at the box and then at him again. He waited patiently and she shook her head as she reached for it. "You shouldn't have. Though I know the words are lost on you."

"Yes, they are. I should have. You really should have whatever you want."

She opened the box and lifted out a watch with a silver band, studded with diamonds. "This is beautiful. It's a gorgeous watch. Thank you so much."

"Thank you, Ava. You've changed our lives completely." He raised his glass. "One more toast—to one of the best teachers ever, a beautiful woman, an unselfish, caring soul."

She touched her glass with his. "Thank you. I'm touched, and the gifts are overwhelming."

"Enjoy them. You've helped Caroline immeasurably. If she can escape her world of silence and sorrow, I can't tell you what it will mean to me and my family and, of course, to her."

"She's the sweetest little girl, Will."

"I think so. I loved my brother, and I want to do this for him and for her. He trusted me with her care, and I've felt as though I've failed him terribly every day since his accident—until today. Today, because of you, I felt I was living up to Adam's trust in me. That's important."

Impulsively, she placed her hand over his. "I know it is."

"You're important, Ava," he said in a husky voice, wrapping his hand around hers.

Candlelight and torchlight flickered across his face, highlighting his strong cheekbones and straight nose, throwing his cheeks in dark shadows. His eyes were midnight, impossible to tell his thoughts. Slipping her hand away from his, she looked away. Her appetite had fled. Desire was a raging fire, burning away everything else.

She picked at her salad, knowing she should eat and should try to get him out of her mind. She looked at the beautiful watch. The small diamonds glittered in the yellow lights. The night was surreal: his yacht; a sexy, breathtaking man; gifts of diamonds and emeralds. A night such as she had never known. How could she continue to resist his charm and seduction?

"Now I really do have a penny for your thoughts," he said in a deep voice, leaning toward her.

"No, I will never tell you. It would definitely go to your head."

"At least that's good news. You're not eating."

"Yes, I am, and it's delicious."

Standing, he came around to hold her chair. "I think we

have time now for that tour of my yacht. We'll come back to dinner."

When she stood, he took her hand. His hand was warm, enveloping hers. "I suspect we are ruining a wonderful dinner by leaving now," she said.

"No, we won't. Neither one of us is particularly hungry. You've barely eaten a bite. Wait until you work up an appetite."

Hunger had fled because she was fluttery over him— something she would never admit.

"So tell me about your yacht."

They entered a glass elevator to go down two decks. When they emerged, he steered her into a passageway. "I'll show you my cabin." He entered an elegant room that was as comfortable and outfitted as some of the living areas in his mansion.

As he turned her to face him, she drew a deep breath. He stood inches away and his dark eyes conveyed desire that set her heart racing. Wrapping his arms around her, he drew her into his embrace to kiss her.

She was lost from the first look into his eyes. She closed her eyes, wrapped her arms around him and kissed him in return, reaffirming the excitement that simmered between them and her own longing. How long since they had last kissed?

Eons, it seemed to her. She stood on tiptoe, kissing him passionately, holding him tightly.

"Ava, this is paradise," he whispered. "It's right and perfect for you to be here in my arms."

She felt the same, yet she had sense enough to know it was all an illusion that would vanish. For the moment it didn't matter. She wanted his kisses and wanted to kiss him in return.

Her heart pounded and she clung to him tightly. "Will,"

she whispered, and then her mouth was on his again as she kissed him passionately.

She wanted him, longed to touch and kiss and explore. Warnings and caution were not heeded. She needed, just once, to do what she wanted because this chance wouldn't come around again. She was already in love with him, part of his life for now. He had opened up opportunities for her, and maybe that was the most he could give of himself.

She ran her fingers in his thick hair, caressing his nape, sliding her hand down the strong column of his neck.

His hands were at the fastening of her dress. He pulled open the zipper and cool air brushed her shoulders. While he continued kissing her, Will pushed away the dress, letting it fall softly around her ankles.

His hands were deft, light, warm on her as he caressed her back, his other arm still circling her waist.

She moaned softly with pleasure, relishing his caresses, pushing away his jacket, playing her hand over the width of his powerful shoulders. Clothing was a barrier. She wanted to explore and discover. She undid his tie while he caressed and distracted her, but finally the tie slid away and she began methodical work on his buttons.

"This is where we should be," he whispered, showering kisses on her temple, her mouth, her cheeks then down her throat.

He stepped back to hold her waist while he looked at her. "You take my breath with your beauty," he whispered. "Ava, this is where we were meant to be from that first moment we met in the Austin restaurant. I've wanted you since the first glance into your green eyes. Ah, love, you're perfection," he said.

His words spun more magic while his hands were everywhere, feathery caresses that heightened desire. She moaned, closing her eyes, yielding to sensations that seduced. He peeled away her flimsy undergarments.

"My necklace—" she whispered.

"Leave it on. When you look at it you'll remember wearing it tonight when I made love to you for the first time. Diamonds for your heart, emeralds for your green eyes. I want you to wear it and nothing else."

Her heart drummed and she kissed him, holding him tightly, knowing she would always remember tonight.

"Just tonight we love," she whispered, wondering if he heard her or believed her. Could she live up to her own declaration?

"Tonight, love." He unfastened the clasp to her bra and pushed it off. His hands cupped her breasts, his thumbs playing over taut peaks and sending an onslaught of tingles. She trembled with desire, wanting him, her fingers tugging free his buttons and pulling off his shirt. She caressed his sculpted chest, the muscles rock-hard beneath her fingers, and then slid her hand down his smooth back. She trailed kisses on his neck while her hands worked free his belt and then his trousers that fell around his ankles. He stepped out of them, taking her with him to leave all of their clothes piled behind while they kissed.

A night to remember. A night to regret. Except at this moment there was no discontent, only joy and abandon. Since she had moved into his mansion, she had been living with his zest for life and supreme hope for what he wanted. He was filled with energy and vitality that added to his appeal.

Her hands played lightly over him and then kisses followed along his shoulder, moving lower while her hands pushed away his briefs to free him.

He was hard, ready for love. He pulled her close to kiss her while she clung to him tightly, feeling as if she were spinning away.

Hot, aching for his touches and kisses, she stroked his hard thighs, feeling tight hair curl against her palm. He was muscled, his legs firm, as sculpted as his chest.

His thick rod pressed against her. He rubbed against her, hot and hard, making her moan with need. She spread her legs and slid his throbbing manhood between them, a taunting pressure, fanning desire into a hotter blaze.

She bent down to kiss him, her tongue tormenting him, teasing him and stirring her more. She took him in her mouth, her tongue playing over him.

He gasped and pulled her up, carrying her as he strode through an open door. He kissed her hand. She wrapped her arm around his neck, relishing each moment, each kiss and touch. She was in love. Nothing could come of it, but there was no denying it. For now, she was close to him, cherished by him, loving him, soon one with him. Intimacy shared would be remembered forever by her.

"I want you," she whispered, more to herself than to him.

"Love, how I want you. You can't begin to imagine," he said. Her heart pounded with joy. Whether his words were meaningless or not, they were being said tonight to her and she wanted to accept them as real, as something he meant with all his heart. "I want to kiss you and love you all this night."

Yanking back the cover, he placed her on the bed and knelt beside her to shower kisses, starting at her ankle and moving up the inside of her leg. Slow, tantalizing, his erotic kisses built need. His hands played lightly, higher, teasing and provoking her.

Her hips writhed as she spread her legs to give him access. Feeling the smooth, hard muscles, she stroked his wide, strong shoulders.

Soft moans were dim in her ears. Unaware of her own voice, she heard only her pounding pulse while sweet torment grew as he moved higher to stroke the inside of her thighs.

She could stand no more and sat up to pull him to her, but his fingers splayed out against her belly and he gently pushed her back to the bed.

Black locks of his hair had fallen over his forehead and the look in his eyes was as volatile as his kisses.

"Will, I want you…." she whispered.

"I want you to desire me with every fiber of your being. This night is special, ours to savor," he said in a husky voice.

Tracing his fingers on her inner thighs, he followed with light kisses, making her want more of him.

"Will," she whispered. Her eyes were shut tightly, all her focus on sensation while she writhed with longing.

His tongue trailed along her inner thigh, hot, wet, another deeper feeling that stirred more need. When his fingers touched her intimately, she gasped with pleasure.

"Will, come here," she said, starting to sit up again only to have him push gently once more.

"Wait, love. Let me pleasure you the way I want. Wait—"

His hand slipped between her thighs. "There, that's what you want, isn't it?" he whispered, coming down beside her, turning on his side to kiss her. His leg was between hers, opening hers and giving him access to her, his fingers still driving her wild with building tension.

"Will—" she gasped again. Her words ended as his mouth covered hers to kiss her passionately while his fingers built a raging fire.

"Let me kiss you," she whispered, pushing him on his back and moving over him, leaning down to circle his nipple with her tongue, excited by the hard peak that made her tingle with awareness of her own.

She moved lower, her tongue flicking over the muscles of his stomach. He quivered beneath her kisses and groaned, his hands winding in her hair.

Caressing him, her fingers stroked sculpted muscles. She closed her hand around his rod to take a lick and tease, rubbing against him.

With a groan, he sat up in a rush, turning her so he was over her. He moved between her legs.

"Will, wait—I'm not protected."

Climbing off the bed, he retrieved a packet from the bedside table. Dim light highlighted his sculpted muscles. Just watching him, tingling, she stayed aroused.

His manhood was hard, ready. He returned to kiss her, pulling her up into his arms, wrapping her in his embrace. "You're special, Ava. You've changed my life," he whispered.

Her heart slammed against her ribs with his words. If only he meant what he said. She clung to him tightly, her eyes squeezed closed as if she could shut herself away from hurt and disaster. She loved him; Will was sexy, handsome, but his caring ways, his gentleness captured her heart so much more. She wanted to kiss him, love him and pour out expressions of her feelings for him, but she couldn't. Declarations of love had to stay locked away because he didn't want them. He wouldn't be able to return them. If he could, it would change the future when they would part to each pursue their goals and dreams.

Instead of speaking, she poured her feelings into her kisses, touching his strong body, wanting him.

"Will," she whispered, biting off the words that were almost spoken. He put on the condom and moved between her legs.

She wrapped her long legs around him and held him tightly as he lowered himself and eased into her. The man she loved she held against her heart. That was another miracle. She had never expected to love again.

Thrusting her hips to meet him, she gasped as she held him, closing her eyes while he slowly entered and filled her.

"Will," she whispered his name again, always stopping before she voiced her feelings aloud. She was afraid if she said even the slightest hint of loving him, all the pent-up longing would tumble out. Her admiration, her desire for Will had become constant in her life.

Desire heightened. They moved together, united and she

was one with him. A moment shared in total intimacy that she could remember as long as she lived.

He was beaded with sweat, slowing to pleasure her, taking his time. She cried out, clutching him tightly.

As his control slipped, they became frenzied, driven, hungry for each other. Stars exploded behind her closed eyes and her pulse roared, drowning out all other sounds. Her faint moans seemed to come from a distance.

She climaxed, rapture carrying her away, losing all sense of reality, as if Will was her entire world. She soared in ecstasy, feeling him shudder while he held her tightly, pumping with his release. "Ava, my love!" he cried.

The endearment was from passion. Words she shouldn't count on to hold meaning, yet joy poured over her. If only the relationship between them could have a future.

Holding each other, they slowed. She still felt wrapped in intimacy with him, clinging to him as he rolled them on their sides. He stroked long, damp strands of her hair from her face while he showered her with light kisses. Encompassed in euphoria, she treasured the moment, so briefly feeling her love returned by him.

"My love, you're perfection. I want make love to you now more than ever. You fulfill dreams and desire. You can't know what you do to me or how exciting you are. You're special in so many ways," he said.

With their hot bodies pressed tightly together, their touching, kisses and endearments, she felt cherished. Her sentiments for him were reflected in his outpourings and caresses for her.

"Will, this is paradise, but it's also a dream that will disappear," she whispered.

"Not for a time. I'm not letting you go anytime soon, so forget that, Ava," he whispered, his tongue following the curve of her ear.

His body was hot, damp, covered with a sheen of sweat,

yet she relished the feel of him, the hard planes, the smooth bulge of muscles, the crisp short hairs on his chest and legs. Stubble was beginning to grow slightly on his jaw. Everything about him was a marvel to her, unique, unforgettable.

She had been in love with him before. Now after passion and sex, she was rapturous, sinking deeper into love, finding him all the more appealing after making love. Will had her heart now—she had given it to him along with her body. This is what she had worried about, but it was too late to turn back.

His dark brown eyes conveyed a warmth that imbued more pleasure. They smiled at each other, the moment of happiness shared.

"I want to hold you close to my heart."

She bit back the words she wanted to say, knowing she couldn't. Instead, she held him quietly, caressing him, kissing him lightly.

He stood and picked her up to shower together. As soon as they dried, they loved again. Afterward, she rose up on one elbow to look down at him while her fingers played lightly across his chest.

"Will, we have to get back to Dallas tonight."

"We could call and fly in tomorrow."

His tempting suggestion hung in the air.

Nine

She shook her head. "No. We said we'd be back and I have to be. This has been a moment, something that happened tonight only. I have to get back and you should, too. We need to return and be there for Caroline."

Smiling at her, he pulled her down to kiss her. Her heart drummed. She longed to wrap her arms around him and forget everything else, but she couldn't. She had had her moment and it was over. It had to be. To prolong what they'd shared would only make her want things she couldn't have.

She sat back to look at him and swung her legs out of bed, pulling a cover up over herself. "I need to get dressed."

He drew her close to look into her eyes and smile. "We made promises, but I would rather stay here for days to make love to you."

"We can't do that. That leads to complications neither of us want. We stop now. Our moment is over, Will. We can't go back there."

"Shh. You don't know that. It was paradise, something special. Don't deny that. I know you felt it."

"Yes, I did, but there are factors and responsibilities. I can't get deeply involved while you don't want to."

"Don't rush to conclusions," he said, smiling at her. "We didn't plan this, yet it happened and the night has been wonderful. You're marvelous. Don't close doors on joy."

She moved away from him, gathering her things. "I'll shower first." She faced him and could see the desire that his brown eyes revealed unmistakably. She half expected him to stop her, but when she shut herself in the shower she was alone.

When she came out, he was nowhere in sight. She finished dressing, combing her long hair and letting it fall free rather than putting it up again.

She wanted him more than ever. Tonight she had crossed a line that would complicate her life for the rest of the summer. Now when she left him at the end of August, it would be a bigger tug on her heart, yet she was beginning to be willing to take chances. Maybe being with Will was changing her.

Leaving Caroline would be another tug on her heart strings.

After a knock, Will entered. Her heart thudded as if she hadn't spent the past hours in his arms with his naked body pressed against hers.

He walked up to her. "You look gorgeous," he said. He ran his fingers through her hair while he leaned close to kiss her lightly in the V of her dress, his tongue stroking her bare skin.

Heat flashed in her, an instant fire. She placed her hands on his arms, holding him, inhaling deeply as she raised her mouth to his and he kissed her.

When he began to caress her, she stepped away. "Will, we can't make love again tonight."

His eyes declared otherwise, giving her a smoldering

denial of her statement, but he took her arm, lacing it in his as they left the cabin.

"I'll feed you. I'm not taking you back with no dinner. Perhaps now we've worked up appetites. Hunger for food. I definitely have a craving for love."

"We'll eat dinner, dance and return to Dallas as we planned and told everyone we would."

Would she ever see Will the same way she had before they had made love? He looked even more handsome as they took the elevator to the top deck.

At their table she held her wrist in the candlelight so she could see the time. He looked amused and took her wrist and pressed a button on her watch. The face was illuminated in a pale green. Startled, she glanced at him. "It'll be 1:00 a.m. in an hour."

"We have time to eat, dance a little and fly back. While we eat, tell me about your plans for your school."

As she spoke about her hopes and dreams for the school, he listened so intently. He was truly interested and that touched her.

"You're so passionate about this," he said. "Your green eyes sparkle. I would like to put this look in your eyes."

"Maybe you did tonight and you're misconstruing the cause," she answered lightly, flirting with him. Something flickered in the depths of his eyes and creases bracketed his mouth.

"I'll see if I can't keep the sparkle in your beautiful green eyes."

"No, Will. This night is unique. When we return to Dallas, it's over. I have a job with Caroline and that will be my total focus. Passion has been an interlude that shouldn't happen again."

"You can't mean that," he said lightly.

"You don't know me well," she replied, intending to hold

to what she was telling him. "My focus will be totally on Caroline."

She could feel a clash of wills while they gazed into each other's eyes until Will nodded. "I can't argue with that one," he said.

She looked away, drinking water and enjoying the pecan-crusted trout, rice, green beans and hot, flaky dinner rolls they were served.

"The next time we're here, hopefully we'll have enough time for me to show you some sights farther south along the coast."

She didn't point out to him she didn't think she would ever be back. "It's beautiful right here with the lights on shore sparkling on the water."

"I haven't looked. You're all I can see tonight. You take my breath."

She could say the same, but she didn't want to tell him. Will needed no encouragement, and she suspected she had only temporarily caught his attention and in time he would lose interest. His cold, cynical attitude about commitment lingered, and she guessed all his romantic relationships were superficial.

"You look deep in thought, Ava," he said.

"Thinking about you, the night, this summer."

"Forget this summer. Tonight what we've discovered about each other is what's important. C'mon. We'll go to the rail's edge," he said. With an arm around her waist, they strolled to the rail where twinkling lights reflected in shifting streaks across black water. He turned to face her. "Here's the best view of all."

She smiled. "Ridiculous," she said, yet warm pleasure filled her with his compliments and flirting. Torchlight flickered on his features and he looked handsome, more appealing than before they loved. She could step back into his arms and make love all over again.

"We should start home, Will."

"A couple of last dances," he said. He took her hand and they returned to dance slow numbers. Will wrapped her in his arms and moved slowly with her. In spite of her declarations to him, she would remember this night for a long time. It had been special for her. She didn't want it to be, because it wasn't for Will. She loved him senselessly and with no future when she hadn't expected to ever fall in love again.

Dancing with him, relishing the moment, she caressed his neck. When the music ended, she placed her hand on his arm. "We should get back, Will. If we wait longer, the sun will be up and so will others."

He nodded and pulled out his cell to give brief instructions to get the chopper ready for the return to shore. She picked up her purse and they left, stepping into the glass elevator. He pulled her into his arms to kiss her. She wrapped her arms around his neck and kissed him in return, her heart pounding with love, excitement, longing for more.

When the elevator stopped, she finally broke off the kisses. "This is hardly private, Will," she said.

His brown gaze intensified, taking her breath. "I want to take you back to my cabin and make love, fast, now."

She shook her head. "Let's stick to the plan to leave."

"You can't tell me you don't really want the same thing," he said, picking up her wrist with his thumb on a vein.

"You feel my racing pulse. I don't care. We're adhering to our plans."

He inhaled deeply and turned to go with her to the chopper, where he helped her climb inside.

In minutes they were in the air and the lights of the yacht sparkled below. She couldn't keep from reaching over to take Will's hand. Her life had changed—a minuscule change in a way, because she would go on with all her school plans. A monumental change in another because she was in love and that love had grown and solidified. She had given her body to Will along with her heart even though he knew nothing about it. And never would know. She didn't want him to ever learn how she felt because there was no place in her future for him and he had no place in his for her.

Shortly, they were seated in his luxurious jet rushing back to Dallas. She glanced at her fancy new watch and saw they would probably get in at about four in the morning.

She wanted to look in on Caroline when she arrived, but Will would; it was his place to and not hers.

"Thinking about tonight, I hope?" he asked.

"Tonight, tomorrow, all that's happened."

"For a little while, just think about tonight and us. It was special, Ava. Really special. We'll be back in our real worlds all too soon." He took her hand, lacing his fingers in hers.

Her pulse speeded as it always did when they touched. Only now, the slightest contact was more of a fiery brand than ever. Memories were constant and vivid, making her want to be back in his arms. How difficult it was to remain cool, slightly distant while longing tormented her. With him, she felt alive, eager, wrapped in temptation that needed constant vigilance.

"I want you in my lap, but I know you're safer buckled in your seat while we fly."

"I'm definitely where I should be," she answered. He leaned over to place his mouth on hers and in seconds her arms were around him.

As his fingers drifted down over her breast, she caught his hand in hers, holding him and ending the kiss. She was breathless, barely able to talk. "We have to go back where we were as employer and tutor, Will. This is crazy."

"No, it's not. And no, we can't ever go back and forget what happened tonight. I don't want to. I see it in your eyes, feel it in your pulse and know it in your kisses. You're not going to forget what's happened. Don't even hint that you can."

"One thing I can't ever possibly forget—your stunning gifts to me. I still say the necklace and watch are breathtaking and you shouldn't have done any such thing when you're paying me a fortune to work for you. They're beautiful, Will, just spectacular, both of them," she said, looking at her watch and touching the necklace lightly.

"I will find another opera or take you to dinner again soon so you can show them off. By the way, I have a safe at home. If you want, I'll put your necklace in there for you while you're at my house."

She smiled at him. "Yes, I've wondered about taking care of them."

"I hope you'll wear the watch."

"Will, you're generous. I've been doing what you hired me to do."

"And succeeding where all others failed. That requires a big bonus. If you've freed Caroline from her grief, you've done the most wonderful thing possible for her and for me. I can't even begin to convey my gratitude. I don't know whether she'll remember as she grows up—"

"She doesn't need to remember. Let her forget. She'll remember me because I hope to keep in touch with her, but she's so young. Let her forget the hurt as much as she can. She can't ever truly forget, but this world of silence she lived in, if she can forget that, let her."

"Damn straight, I will. I hope you're always in touch with her."

Did he really mean that? In touch with Caroline meant in touch with Will. She suspected women he had made love to eventually went out of his life and he rarely gave them a thought once they were gone.

The pilot announced their approach to Dallas and soon they touched down in a smooth landing.

In a short time they climbed the stairs in his silent mansion. When they reached her door, he stepped inside and closed the door before drawing her into his embrace. The moment he kissed her, her heart thudded. Longing mushroomed while she wrapped her arms around his neck and kissed him passionately. Why did his kisses seem right, so necessary?

His tongue went deep, stroking hers. Pulling her up against him, he kissed her hard, possessively. While they kissed, he swept her into his arms to carry her across the room. When he stood her on her feet, she wriggled away.

Rampant desire tore at her. "Will, it's time to say goodnight. We've come back to life like it was. I'm committed to Caroline and then leaving for my teaching. I don't want to complicate my life with an affair."

"I'd say you already have," he whispered, caressing her cheek. She caught his hand to kiss his palm, her actions denying her words.

"Good night," she whispered and moved away from him. "You have to go now," she said.

The force of the desire in his expression shook her. As they locked gazes, tension grew until he turned away. He closed the door quietly behind him.

She touched the necklace around her throat. "I love you, Will Delaney," she whispered. She walked to the mirror to look at the magnificent necklace he had given her. She couldn't imagine the cost of it. Touching it with awe as she stared at it, she found it impossible to realize it was actually hers.

Placing it carefully on the dresser, she looked at sparkling diamonds and the glittering emeralds that glowed in brilliant green. She unfastened the watch to place it beside the necklace. Both pieces of jewelry were gorgeous, lavish and breathtaking. It was impossible to grasp they were really hers, especially the fabulous necklace.

Keyed up, she crawled into bed to be enveloped in memories of hours earlier with Will and their lovemaking.

The room was growing light when Ava fell asleep and then she overslept. She rushed to get dressed and grabbed a hasty glass of orange juice with a piece of toast before she left to search for Caroline, expecting to find her with Rosalyn, who usually left Will's mansion as soon as Ava took charge.

Ava hurried toward the playroom. Just outside the open door, she paused when she heard Will's voice. Her heart skipped at the sound of Caroline's laughter.

"Muffy's cute, Uncle Will." Caroline giggled. "Thank you for Muffy." Ava started to enter, but stopped when Will spoke.

"Remember Miss Ava is the one who first thought you might like a puppy, so you should thank Miss Ava, too."

"I will. Miss Ava is my friend," came a childish voice Ava had rarely heard. Caroline's statement gave Ava joy. "Is she your friend, Uncle Will?"

"Yes, she is, Caroline."

"I don't want her to leave," Caroline said and then squealed. Ava heard Muffy's growl and knew the pup was playing with either Caroline or Will.

Ava walked quietly into the room. Sitting cross-legged on the floor in chinos and a black knit shirt, Will pulled on a dog toy held by Muffy, who shook it. He was laughing along with Caroline. Suddenly he let go and Muffy sat on her haunches, staring at them with the toy hanging in her mouth.

Caroline grabbed the toy and the tug-of-war began again. Once more Ava was touched by Will's care for his niece.

"I overslept," Ava said, feeling her cheeks grow warm at Will's knowing smile.

"Imagine that," he said and she gave him a look.

Caroline squealed when Muffy jerked the toy out of her hands. She laughed, getting up and running to Ava to hug her. Startled, Ava picked up Caroline. She smelled sweet and was soft, her skin as smooth as rose petals. "Thank you, Miss Ava, for wanting me to have Muffy."

Ava hugged her. "You're very welcome. I'm so glad you like Muffy."

Caroline played with a long lock of Ava's hair. "I love Muffy." She looked at the pup and Ava set her on her feet. The minute she touched the floor she ran to play with the pup. Muffy chased her and Caroline ran away with Muffy nipping at her heels.

Will stood and crossed to Ava. "Good morning."

"Thanks for letting me sleep."

"I wanted to wake you, but I didn't." He ran his finger along her cheek. "You look as if you had a full night's sleep. There are all sorts of things I'd like to do this morning, but I know I can't," he whispered, still in a thick, husky tone that kept her thinking of their night together.

"Just as well, Will," she said, trying to get her breath.

"It's been a fun morning with Caroline. Ava, she's coming out of that shell completely. At least when she plays with the dog. You see how she does with her reading. It's just fantastic what a difference one little mutt can make."

"That little mutt means so much to her," Ava said,

"I'll leave you with her and the pup. I think the baby is getting tired," he said. She looked around to see Muffy stretched on the floor and Caroline petting her. The little dog blinked and closed her eyes while Caroline tried to entice her to play more.

"See you later, Will," Ava said.

"It'll be more than just 'seeing,'" he said in a husky voice. She couldn't wait.

Will left for his office to make two calls, the first to Zach, to tell him the news about Caroline, the second to Ryan.

"Zach, it's Will. I know you got the attorney's letter about the will—the reading is scheduled for two weeks from now."

"It's on my calendar," Zach answered. "How's Caroline?"

"She's coming out of her silence. I mean really out."

"Hallelujah," Zach yelled loudly enough Will had to hold the phone away from his ear as he laughed.

"I wanted to shout, too. It's fantastic."

"That's the best possible news, Will. That's the greatest. I haven't been any help, but I care."

"I know you do."

"What happened? Was it the new teacher you hired?"

"Yes. Ava suggested I get her a puppy. A pup is hard to resist. It was almost instant."

"Damn, that's good news."

"You're going to be surprised when you see her, Zach."

"I'll go get something for her and this pup."

Will leaned back to talk to his brother, next calling Ryan, happy to tell each of them about Caroline. When he finished his calls, he sat thinking about Ava. He wanted to whisk her away, somewhere he could be alone with her and make love to her endlessly. Last night had been spectacular. No woman had ever excited him the way she did, and he didn't want to let her go. Instead, she didn't even want to go out again. He raked his fingers through his hair. He wanted to be alone with her to make love to her tonight. But it wasn't going to happen, he was certain. She was driven, determined, bright, accustomed to getting her way—unfortunately some of the same qualities he possessed. It was his stand on commitment and marriage that held her back. Would commitment to Ava be a silken trap the way Adam's marriage had been for him?

Will thought about life with Ava, and it appealed to him in a way the thought of a long-term—actually lifetime—commitment had never appealed before. Was Ava changing him? Or was he changing to keep her in his life? He didn't want to think about life without her. He was like Caroline: he didn't want Ava to leave. Did he want her badly enough to think about marriage?

Or was this the kind of fuzzy, blinded-by-love thinking that had tied Adam into a rotten marriage?

* * *

During dinner on the veranda, Will asked, "How were the books and reading today?"

He saw Ava and Caroline exchange a look, and he put down his roll and butter knife. "What's this?

"Caroline read so very well today," Ava said. "She answered my questions correctly, read a second-grade book and she told me she'd read to you tonight."

Will's heart thudded and he forgot his dinner. "That's fantastic," he said, looking at Caroline, who smiled broadly.

"You should have told me before dinner. You should have called me this afternoon. I can't wait to have you read to me," he said, meaning it. Joy filled him and it was difficult to keep quiet and act natural. He wanted to scoop up Caroline, hug and kiss her and shout for glee. Emotions shook him and he tried to get his voice and stay casual. He leaned closer to Caroline. "Sweetie, I am so proud of you and so happy to hear what you read."

She smiled at him.

"Thank you," he said to Ava, wanting to pull her into his arms. He wanted to hug both of them. He had lost his appetite, but Caroline was eating and Ava had taken a bite, so he knew he shouldn't disrupt their dinners.

He sipped his water. "Tell me about one of the books you read, Caroline."

To his astonishment, she began a story. Again he shot Ava a grateful glance. She had worked a miracle in no time. A little dog had worked a miracle, too. He put down his fork, listening closely to Caroline tell him about a story she read earlier in the day. It was not one he recalled reading to her, so it wasn't an old favorite or one she was already familiar with. More than ever, he wanted to shout for joy, but he was afraid he might intimidate his niece.

"Sweetie, what a fun story. You did an excellent job telling me about it. That's fantastic. I'm glad you liked it. Is this one of the books Miss Ava gave you?"

"Yes, sir," Caroline answered, and again his heart squeezed with relief and happiness.

After dinner, Ava sat in a rocker in the upstairs playroom, watching Caroline sitting on Will's lap, reading to him. Though he listened intently, Will would occasionally glance at Ava with a joyous expression that filled her with happiness.

He misplaced all the credit he gave her for Caroline's transformation. It was far more about the little ball of fur who was currently stretched out asleep, but Ava was happy for him and for Caroline. He had said he wasn't good daddy material, but he was patient and considerate with Caroline—so wrong about himself. He had been emotional at dinner over the change in Caroline, and Ava was touched, sharing his joy.

"Caroline, that is grand. You are such a smart little girl," Will said as she finished reading to him. She slipped off his lap and ran to plop beside Muffy, waking the pup while she petted her.

"Uncle Will and Miss Ava, let's play a game," Caroline said. "I'll take Muffy outside for a minute while you set up the game."

"I'll come with you." Will held Muffy while Caroline skipped beside him as they left.

Ava chose one from a closet filled with toys and games. She placed the board game on the floor, and when Will and Caroline returned, they all sat around it to play. She was constantly aware of Will being attentive to Caroline, giving her his full attention.

Watching Caroline, Ava marveled at the change that had been so quick. When they finished two rounds of the game,

Will asked Caroline if she wanted to see a movie and suggested she get ready for bed first.

"I want Miss Ava to help me get ready for bed," Caroline said.

Ava nodded and Will left to take Muffy out again.

Later, Caroline curled in Will's lap while the three sat on the sofa to watch a movie. Rosalyn came in to view the movie with them. Ava noticed when Caroline began to nod and shortly she was asleep. Will paused the movie to carry Caroline to bed.

Ava went outside. The evening was beginning to cool. Lights were on the veranda and pool. Finally Will returned, pulling her up into his arms to kiss her hard.

Her heart slammed against her ribs the moment he drew her into his embrace. Then she closed her eyes, clinging to him to return his kiss. When she started to move away, he held her with his arm around her waist. "I want you in my arms. I want to make love to you."

His husky voice was as tantalizing as a caress. She longed to follow her heart and kiss him. Instead, she held his forearms, feeling the solid muscles. "Will, we're not getting more involved," she whispered, her heartbeat racing.

"I'd say we're already involved, darlin'." As his arm tightened around her, she resisted. He leaned closer to kiss her again, but she pulled away.

"Will, you're not listening to me. We're not having an affair. I'm doing a job with Caroline, which I think is phasing out rapidly. Her reading is beyond kindergarten level." Ava took a deep breath. All the time she talked, Will showered kisses on her temple, cheek and down to her throat.

He raised his head to look into her eyes and she couldn't move or talk. Her heart pounded while her lips tingled. Desire enveloped her, a hunger that erased everything else.

"No," she whispered, her protest feeble, far more faint than all her words had been. Will placed his lips on hers and kissed her, his tongue stroking hers. She trembled, standing stiffly for only a moment and then melting. She kissed him passionately as if starved for his loving. As her hands swept over him, he picked her up and carried her inside the cabana, kicking closed the door in the bedroom. Clothes were tossed away. When she fumbled with the buttons on his shirt, Will ripped it away, buttons popping. He yanked open her shirt, pushing it off along with her bra. They kissed while they undressed each other. Standing in front of her, he lifted her up and she wrapped her long legs around him, winding her fingers in his hair while her other hand pressed against his muscled back. Her heart pounded with desire and joy. This is where she longed to be, dreamed about—in Will's arms.

He lowered her on his thick rod and she gasped with pleasure as they loved with desperate urgency. She wanted him with a deep need that consumed her. Loving him was a necessity. She cried out in ecstasy when she climaxed as he pumped furiously and shuddered with his release.

Clinging to him, she slowed while rapture wrapped her in euphoria.

She kissed his shoulder lightly and soon he shifted her. When she stood, he picked her up to carry her to the bed, yanking away the covers. He lay down beside her and pulled her into his arms.

He combed her hair from her face. "I've wanted you so badly, you're all I think about," he said gruffly. Her heartbeat quickened in response to his words and the look in his eyes.

"I wasn't going to do that again. Will, we're going where I wanted to avoid from the start."

"I didn't notice a lot of reluctance on your part just now," he whispered. "Ava, this is good between us. It seems right, inevitable from the first moment. Go with what you want."

"Maybe you can move from relationship to relationship so easily, but I can't. To say the least. I need commitment. For all your wealth, that's something you can't give me. Making love is an intimate, binding event. I can't deal with it without commitment."

"We are both dealing quite well," he said, showering kisses on her face, her lips and throat.

"Will, are you even listening to me?"

"Of course. You're amazing, fantastic. I've never known a woman like you. You're the sexiest woman ever," he whispered. "Your kisses burn me to embers."

She wanted to put her hands over her ears. His words were golden chains that could hold her heart captive. She kissed him lightly, just to stop the compliments. She rolled away and stood. "Will, I'm dressing and going in. Otherwise, we'll make love all night long."

"Which is the best possible idea," he said, propping himself on his elbow and looking at her as she stood nude before him. She turned away and grabbed up his shirt to yank it on. "I'll borrow this for a minute so I'm covered," she said, picking up her other clothes.

"The view was much better before you found my shirt. Ava, come here," he said in a husky, coaxing tone that curled her toes and stirred desire again.

Without looking back, she clutched her things and rushed for the door. "I'll dress and go, Will. You stay right where you are," she flung over her shoulder, pulling on clothes as she went. There were two bedrooms, a living area with a bar, and bathrooms in the cabana, but she yanked on her things and dropped his shirt in the hall. She hurried out and across the veranda, half expecting Will to stop her at any moment.

In her room she closed the door and leaned against it. She had to find other arrangements for the evenings. She couldn't be alone with Will night after night and still avoid succumbing to his seductive ways.

She pulled out her laptop to search for condos or apartments in the area. She would finish her time with Caroline, but she had to move out of Will's mansion and get away from him before she moved into his bed for an affair that would last until Will walked away. Each time they had made love, she was more deeply in love with him, her heart bound to him more. She couldn't imagine a time when she wouldn't love him, whether she was with him or away from him, but if there was any hope of getting over him, now was the time to move away. He talked about her being special and said wonderful endearments, but there was no commitment from him, nor would there be. The sooner she moved on, maybe the less she would be hurt.

Ten

In the morning Ava dressed in a black shirt and black capris with sandals. When she went down to breakfast, she heard Will's deep voice and another male voice in the dining room.

"Ava," Will said as she approached the doorway. "Come meet my brother Zach Delaney. Zach, meet our wonder teacher, Ava Barton."

Zach extended his hand. "I'm honored to meet you and tell you we owe you a far bigger thanks than we can ever convey."

She shook his warm, calloused hand. "I've had plenty of thanks, and I'm so happy for the change in Caroline. She's a little sweetheart," Ava said, surprised to face a man whose looks were different from his brother. Her gaze ran swiftly over Zach's rugged features, a craggy jaw, his startling blue eyes, a total contrast to Will's dark brown eyes. "I don't believe I'd pick you out in a crowd as Will's brother. I can't see that you resemble each other at all."

Both grinned. "Thank heavens for that," Will remarked

about two seconds before Zach expressed the same sentiment and Ava had to chuckle.

"Please have a seat, Ava," Will said, holding a chair for her. As soon as she sat, both men did.

"I've been telling Zach about last night. All of it was a miracle. Everything Caroline did—her talking and joining in. She ate a good dinner. She reads well, far better now than she used to. She initiated a game with us, then wanted us to watch a movie with her."

Zach smiled at Ava. "You really are a miracle for this family. You may get tired of hearing that, but I know how hard Will tried before he found you."

"I think a lot of credit goes to a little puppy," Ava said.

The brothers both shook their heads.

"Each one of those things is a miracle—all of them to-gether—this change blows my mind," Will said, sipping his coffee. He turned to Ava. "We've finally gotten letters from Dad's lawyer that we'll have a reading of Dad's will in two weeks. Zach and Ryan will both be here. There won't be any surprises, unless Adam's wife gets her hopes up, which she should know better. Dad never liked her after she and Adam began having trouble."

"I suppose Mom will be there," Zach said.

"I can't imagine her missing this. I'll call her, but she's on the same list we are."

"She'll fly in, hear what she already knows, take us to lunch and go. Heaven knows when we'll see her again."

"Think she'll come see Caroline?" Ava asked.

"She's not the doting grandmother. I seriously doubt it. The plans now are to read the will at his office."

"Will, I can't imagine," Ava said. "Is Caroline going to miss her when she doesn't see her?"

"No. They aren't close—surprise, surprise," Zach said with a cynical note in his voice. "My brother may not have told you, but marriages in this family have not worked out well."

"I don't think Lauren will show. I think our ex-sister-in-law will send her attorney," Will said with a cold tone in his voice that chilled Ava. "Dad told me he left her the token one dollar so she can't declare she was forgotten. She won't come and she won't want to see Caroline."

"I still can't imagine. Such a precious child," Ava said.

Zach glanced at his watch, finished his coffee and stood. "I have to go. Both of you, stay where you are. Ava, it was great to meet you. Endless thanks to you," he said, shaking hands once again with her.

As Will left to walk out with Zach, all Ava could think about was the Delaney family—and how glad she was that Caroline had wonderful uncles who cared deeply about her.

Ava had another productive day with Caroline. After lessons ended for the afternoon, she had business to take care of, and when Rosalyn arrived to replace her, she summoned a limo and left the mansion.

It was past six o'clock when she returned, but it wasn't until after Caroline went to bed that Ava saw her opportunity to talk to Will. She found him in the downstairs family room.

He had changed to jeans and a T-shirt, his legs stretched out comfortably on the sofa.

"You said you wanted to talk. I've been curious all evening what this concerns. Come sit here by me. I don't bite hard," he added with a faint smile.

She moved to the far end of the sofa and he gave her a mocking look.

"Will, I plan to work with Caroline all summer as we agreed."

"So where is this going?" he asked, sipping his cold beer.

"That means I will work every weekday with Caroline

until six. Then Rosalyn will take over or you'll be here. Today I leased a condo near here for the rest of the summer."

His expression didn't change as he looked at her intently. "Why?"

"I think you can figure why. I've told you from the start, I can't handle an affair. I also have found that I can't say no to you, so I'm moving where temptation will not be as great. It won't affect my work with Caroline at all."

"I don't want you to go," he stated, and the words twisted her heart. She wanted to scream at him that she didn't want to leave, either, but she had to, or else see her heart broken far worse later. "This place is big enough—move into the other wing and we'll never see each other after six if you want. I'll take care of your lease."

"No," she said, trying to hang on to patience. "I'm not moving to a different part of your house."

"This will set Caroline back."

"No, it won't. I'll talk to her about it tomorrow, and if it seems in any way to upset her, then I'll rethink my plans. I think I can put it to her so she won't mind and she'll never notice. I'll stay for dinner sometimes if I'm invited, and into early evenings with the two of you, but I'll have my own place to go to and we will not have a repeat of last night."

"And that was so terrible?"

"You know it was not," she said. "That's the problem. It was wonderful."

"Ava, damnit," he said, moving beside her and slipping his hand behind her hair. "You can't tell me our loving was wonderful and you're moving to get away from me in the same breath."

"You'll break my heart. I can't deal with a casual affair. Or even a serious one. I'd want marriage. There isn't a future for us."

"I'm not asking for a future. Just a day at a time in the here and now."

"That's the problem, Will. Can't you see? I'm not a 'day at

a time' person. I want it all. I want commitment. I want your love for all time. I can't give you a day at a time, and I've told you as much from the first." She stood. "Now, in the interest of keeping this a professional relationship from here on, I'll say good-night."

He came to his feet to wrap his arms around her.

"Will—"

He kissed away the rest of her words. His hands were everywhere, caressing her back, her bottom, unfastening her slacks and pushing them away.

She pressed lightly against his chest. Continuing to kiss her, his hands went beneath her blouse to cup her breasts and he played over her nipples, stroking her, destroying her rising protests. She couldn't say no. In seconds, her hands moved over him while she caressed him and he picked her up to carry her to a bedroom, closing the door.

Later, when she lay against him, held tightly in his arms, she ran her fingers through the mat of curls on his chest. "This is exactly why I have the condo."

"It won't change things except be more inconvenient sometimes for you," he predicted. "You'll see."

"Will, you're not listening to what I'm saying."

"Of course, I am. It's just ridiculous when this is what you want."

"Don't push."

"This is the best, Ava. The very best," Will said in husky tones. He pulled her closer and kissed her lightly. Her heart sank. It would be so difficult to move, and in spite of her cheerful front with Will, she hated having to tell Caroline that she was moving.

"I can't do this, Will. I really can't."

"I think you do it supremely well," he said, nuzzling her neck and she gave up talking to him about it, turning to kiss him instead.

She was still moving, though.

* * *

The next afternoon after she was finished with teaching, Ava was stretched on the floor with Caroline as she worked on a puzzle.

"Caroline, I love being here with you and your uncle Will, but I'm going to move into my place nearby."

Caroline looked up and worry clouded her brown eyes while her brow furrowed. "You're moving away?"

"I'm moving very close by. I will still be here when you get up in the morning, and I'll stay until dinner time when Rosalyn comes. Sometimes I'll spend the evening until you go to bed. I don't think you'll notice much difference."

"I won't?" she asked.

"No. And then you'll have a place you can come visit and stay with me all night," Ava said, the words popping out before she had even thought them over.

"I can stay all night with you?"

"Yes."

Tears welled up in Caroline's eyes and she stood, running the few feet to Ava. She threw her arms around Ava and clung tightly. "Don't go."

"I'm really not going except late at night and very early in the morning before you're awake," Ava said, holding the frail little girl. "Don't cry, because you won't notice the difference, and if you do, I promise, I'll move right back in here."

"You promise?" Caroline asked, leaning back to look into Ava's eyes.

Ava pulled out a clean tissue to wipe away Caroline's tears. Her heart was in knots and she had a lump in her throat. "Absolutely. If you don't like it, I do promise to move right back here, so don't cry. If you're not happy with where I've moved, I'll come back. It will be up to you. You know I'll be leaving when the summer is over, but if I have this condo, you'll be able to come visit when you want and I can come visit you every day if you want."

Caroline studied her intently and then nodded her head. "Will you show me where you'll live?"

"Yes, I will. You can come this week and help me arrange my things. How's that?"

Caroline thought for a few long seconds. "I want to do that."

"All right. I'll ask your uncle," Ava replied. "Now a smile."

Caroline smiled and Ava hugged her again, feeling torn in two.

She had fallen in love with two Delaneys—Will and Caroline. She didn't want to move away from either of them. She loved them both, and she hurt. As much as she loved them, she couldn't possibly settle for an affair with no sense of a future. Will would eventually end it. It would be devastating to watch him walk out and later see him going out with someone else.

Ava hugged Caroline lightly again and wiped her eyes swiftly. Caroline scooped up Muffy and returned to where she had been sitting on the floor, with the little brown bear beside her.

When Rosalyn arrived, Ava left, driving to her condo. Silence overwhelmed her in the empty place and she longed to be back at Will's mansion with Will and Caroline. This empty condo was going to get more empty and lonesome by the day, because she missed them terribly and didn't want to move away. She leaned against a blank wall and cried. This wasn't what she wanted in the least.

Two weeks later, on the last Friday in July, Will prepared for the reading of his father's will, dressing in his charcoal suit with a tailor-made white shirt. As he moved around, his gold cuff links glinted in his French cuffs. His mind should be on the reading, seeing his mother and dealing with Lauren's lawyer, but he couldn't stop thinking about Ava.

He hated that she lived elsewhere. She filled most of his

waking hours to the point of distraction. She had not shown him her condo yet, and he tried to keep her at his home every night. He had to admit Caroline was doing all right, but that was because Ava stayed until Caroline went to bed a lot of nights.

He knew Ava still kept some things in her suite at his place for Caroline's benefit.

"Damnit," he swore while trying to get his tie just right. He missed Ava far more than he had expected to, something that surprised him. They had barely had much intimate time together, hardly what anyone would call an affair. He should not give her moving a thought. Instead, he missed her— more than missed her, he hated having her gone. He had never missed anyone before. Usually, he was all right with the parting, but then he was usually the one who walked out of the relationship. With Ava it was so different. He missed their long talks, the companionship with someone who cared about Caroline and understood Caroline's problems and her development. Ava seemed as happy as he and his brothers had been over Caroline's blossoming. And making love with Ava—it had been the best he had ever known.

He gritted his teeth and tried to concentrate on his tie and forget Ava, but he couldn't. She would not have an affair— which left marriage. Something he had always planned to avoid because of his parents' marriage and his brother's. Yet Ava was not materialistic the way Lauren had been, nor was she as socially driven and vain as his mother. Maybe he should not base his own life on his dad's and his brother's.

Was he in love enough for a total commitment?

He yanked the tie free to start all over. He saw Ava about half as much as before. They swam with Caroline, ate dinner with her. The difference was he wasn't alone with Ava. She always had Caroline with her. This was the end of July; in a few short weeks, her job would be over and now, thanks to him, she was financially independent. She would go out of their lives. He needed to talk to her about how that would affect Caroline. And he didn't want her to leave, either.

Finally dressed and ready, he headed to Caroline's room. When he stepped inside, Ava sat on the floor with the girl. Ava's hair was caught behind her head in a clip and she wore a simple sundress and sandals. He ached to go pick her up, carry her back to his room and peel her out of the dress.

Desire burned and he clenched his fist, trying to think of something else. Muffy ran up to greet him and he gave the dog a perfunctory pat. "Good morning," he said, his voice deeper, with a husky note he couldn't keep out.

Caroline smiled at him. "We're playing a game before we read."

Ava smiled. She looked cool, remote and he wondered if she was happy living away from his place.

"You look very nice," she said. "Are you on your way to the attorney's?"

"Yes. Zach and Ryan will come back with me and stay tonight. Garrett will join us for dinner. And Caroline can read for them. If you want to," he added and she smiled and nodded.

"Good girl." He walked over to pick her up, swinging her up in his arms and kissing her cheek. "You look very pretty this morning in your pink shirt and shorts. Muffy's pink collar just matches."

"Muffy had a bath yesterday and she smells good," Caroline said.

"Good. I'm not picking up Muffy in my dark suit, though."

Caroline laughed and he set her down, looking at Ava and meeting her gaze. Desire flared in her green eyes and his heart missed a beat. She was not as cool and remote as she appeared. His pulse speeded. "Will you stay for dinner with us and meet Ryan? He wants to meet you because of your work here."

"Yes, thank you," she said.

"Great," he said. "I'll leave you two to your fun. I'll be home with the guys as soon as we can get loose."

He left, his pulse beating faster. She still responded to him. Moving out hadn't changed much except to make her less accessible. How could he get her back? And keep her here when summer ended? He wanted her back because he could see desire in her green eyes and she was as responsive as ever to him. She should try an affair—for all either one of them knew, it might lead to a long-term commitment. Affairs didn't have to be short.

He swore under his breath. Reasonable or not, he wanted her back in his house and in his bed at night. He missed her in too many ways. He missed holding and kissing her. He missed talking to her. He missed her teasing and laughter. Her concern for Caroline.

"Damnit, Ava," he said in his empty car, "come back home to me."

At twenty minutes before two, Will reached the attorney's office. He was greeted by the receptionist and shown to a room where he could wait. In minutes both Zach and Ryan arrived. He shook hands first with Zach and then turned to his youngest brother, whose dark looks most resembled his own.

"It's good to see you both. The others should arrive anytime now."

"I saw a limo pulling up as we walked into the building," Zach said.

"It could be Mom or it could be Lauren," Ryan added.

"It's probably Mom," Will said.

Zach studied Will. "What the hell's happened to you, Will? Business deal gone sour?"

"Not at all. What are you talking about?"

"You look like hell," he said, and Ryan laughed.

"He's kind of right," Ryan said, tilting his head to look at his older brother.

"I'm fine, and thanks for the notice that I look like hell." Zach continued to stare at Will. "How's the teacher doing?"

"Fine. She'll be there tonight for dinner."

"She lives there, this summer, doesn't she?" Ryan asked.

"She did. She's there all day. She has a nearby condo."

"Since when? She was living there the last I heard," Zach said, still studying his brother.

"Since a few weeks ago," Will said, tiring of the stares and questions. "End of subject."

"I'll be damned," Zach said. "When I was at your house, I recall you telling me about flying her to dinner on your yacht."

"That was a thank-you for what she has done with Caroline," he answered. "Here's Garrett," Will said with relief, turning to extend his hand to his right-hand man. The four tall men stood quietly talking until a short blonde woman swept into the room.

Will marveled again that she was his mother. He could see little physical resemblance in any of them to her. Short with a lush figure and small waist, Lois Sanderson had platinum-blond hair. Her turquoise eyes had not been inherited by any of them, either. She had married twice since their father, but with no children in any other marriage.

"Mother," he said, kissing her offered cheek.

His brothers obediently did the same.

As Garrett greeted her, a man they didn't know entered the room and stood off to one side. He merely nodded at them.

"Your granddaughter is growing," Will said to his mother.

"Ah, Caroline. I'm sorry I won't be able to see her this trip. Perhaps the next one."

"She'll start kindergarten in September."

"I always send her cards on holidays, presents on her birthday. I believe she is five now."

Will kept a smile, but he could only feel annoyance that his mother had so little interest in her granddaughter. He exchanged a look with Zach that obviously conveyed Zach's ire.

Shortly a white-haired man entered, accompanied by two younger men who bore faint resemblances to Will and Ryan: Will's uncle and cousins.

The door to an inner office opened and a man stepped out. "Would all of you like to come in."

They entered a room with chairs set up facing a desk. They took their seats, their mother in the front row with their uncle beside her and his sons beside him.

Will, his brothers and Garrett sat on the next row behind her.

"This shouldn't take long," Zach stated. "I'm ready for that swim and juicy steaks tonight."

More cousins filed into the back of the room and sat. Shortly, Grady Gibson, their father's tall, thin attorney, entered and greeted each one of them, moving around the room before going to the front to start.

"We'll get down to business now. I am reading Argus Delaney's will and each of you has been notified and asked to be present."

He sat and began to read.

Will heard his name read by Grady and listened, remembering when his father had called him and told him about his inheritance, which would increase Will's sizable fortune considerably.

"To my son William Lucius Delaney, I hereby give and bequeath the sum of four billion dollars," Grady read.

Will listened to details and the bequest of the family home, which would eventually revert to Caroline. Zach would get a summer home in Italy. Ryan would get a Colorado home. Garrett would get the ranch.

Next, Grady read Zach's and Ryan's inheritances, equal to Will's. A trust was left for Caroline, to be managed by Will, which he already knew. Grady moved on to Garrett.

Twenty-five million was left to their mother. When Lauren's name was read, the attorney representing her sat straighter. Grady announced the sum of one dollar, and the man stood, striding out of the room and slamming the door. Before he moved on to their father's brother and his family, Grady looked up and his gaze ran over all of them.

Will had returned to thinking about Ava, seated with Caroline in her sundress, so enticing this morning. He wanted to be through with this and get home where she was.

Grady caught Will's eye and Will stopped thinking about Ava. There had to be something unexpected in the will, because Grady was giving them a warning in his own quiet way.

Eleven

Grady won Will's full attention. Will's mind raced, trying to think what else could be in the will.

Grady looked down at the paper spread before him. "To my daughter, Sophia Marie Rivers, I hereby bequeath—"

There was an audible gasp from the beneficiaries. Startled, Will glanced at Zach. "We have a sister?" Zach whispered, leaning in front of Garrett. Will's mother cried out in surprise. She stood, her cheeks flushed.

"Grady, what are you talking about? A daughter? I'm the mother of the only children he had."

"No, Lois, you're not. If you'll be seated, I'll continue reading."

She clamped her mouth closed and sat while his uncle put his arm around her to pat her shoulder.

Zach leaned slightly in front of Garrett to look at Will. "What difference does it make to her now?"

Without answering, Will turned back to listen because Grady waited for quiet. "To my daughter, Sophia Marie

Rivers, I hereby bequeath three billion dollars." Will stiffened at the amount being given to a woman none of them had even known existed.

"In order to bring Sophia into the family," Grady continued, "she is to become a member of the Board of Trustees for the Delaney Foundation. She has one year from the reading of this will to become a member. If she does not become a member of the board, Sophia, as well as my sons, Will, Zach and Ryan, will forfeit their inheritances. If this happens, the money is to be given to the following charities…"

Stunned, Will didn't hear what Grady read. They would have to meet this half sister. Meet and welcome her into the family and get her on the family board.

His head swam. What had his father been thinking?

He turned to look at Zach, who stared back with as much shock in his expression as Will felt. Ryan sat rubbing his jaw, glancing at Will and then at Zach.

His mother cried with a handkerchief to her face while his uncle continued to pat her shoulder.

Sophia Rivers. A stranger they had never met, even if they had the same blood in their veins. Three billion dollars given to her. Shocked, Will wasn't aware of what Grady read.

Sophia Marie Rivers. He, Zach and Ryan had a half sister. How old was she? Who was she? Where did she live? Questions bombarded Will and he didn't hear what Grady read as he got to Will's uncle and the uncle's family.

Finally Grady finished and adjourned, walking around the desk to get to Will before anyone else. "You dropped a bomb," Will said.

"I know, but that's the way he wanted it. I talked to your father about this. Your mother is less than happy, which he expected, and I know she's going to be even less happy when she discovers your half sister's age is the same as Ryan's."

"In other words she was born while Mom and Dad were still married."

"That's right."

"Grady, why did he want to bring her into the family now when we're all grown?"

"I asked him, and he was determined about it. He said it would bring his family together."

"Damnit. He should have brought her into the family years ago if he wanted family togetherness. She might not want this, either. Though I can't see anyone turning away that kind of money. Well, hell. Was he close to her?"

"I couldn't get much out of him about that. I don't think he was. I think she resented him from the way he talked. I know he provided for her and her mother generously all Sophia's life."

"He might as well have had you toss a bomb into the room today. Except if we lived through a bomb, we could get over it. I don't know about this. Grady, Mom is bearing down on you. Come out to the house if you can. We'd be happy to have you."

"Thanks. Sorry to surprise you, but he wanted it that way."

Will shook his head. "My dad. He had an ornery streak."

"Grady," Will's mother said behind the attorney, her voice sharp.

"Sorry, I won't be able to join you, but thanks," Grady said and turned away.

"We have a half sister," Zach said as he, Ryan and Garrett gathered around.

"Did you know about this?" Will asked Garrett, who shook his head.

"No. Absolutely not."

"Why on earth didn't he tell us?" Zach asked. "Or at least tell you?"

Will shrugged. "Maybe he didn't want any criticism or to have to answer questions. I'm surprised she wasn't here, because she had to have been notified about this reading."

"You're right," Zach said. "I'm asking Grady."

"You'll have to get in line behind Mom," Will said.

"I'll catch him," Zach replied, leaving to cross the room to Grady. In minutes he was back. "I asked Grady why she didn't come. She didn't want to. She doesn't want her inheritance."

"If she turns down her inheritance, we lose ours," Ryan said. "That's way too much money to lose. We'll have to talk her into accepting her bequest. Why on earth would she turn down three billion?"

"Because she's angry, most likely," Garrett remarked dryly. "She's obviously illegitimate. You've never heard of her, much less met her."

"She must be enormously wealthy herself," Zach added.

"We'll have to send someone to meet her and talk to her," Will stated. "I can contact her. I'm the oldest, so I should be the one."

"Fine with me," Zach said.

"You know I agree," Ryan added.

"Well, I'm heading home. You guys, come on. We can talk about it at home tonight. Anyone need a ride?" Will asked, but all declined.

He left in long strides, wanting to get home before the others so he could have a few minutes alone with Ava.

Will walked through the house and to the veranda. Ava sat near the pool, watching Caroline play while Muffy slept in her crate. Ava's long hair fell over one shoulder and he wanted to comb his fingers through the silky strands. Sunlight brought out golden highlights.

Will pulled a chair close to hers and sat. "How's it going today?"

"Just great. She's doing so well. I have an appointment to talk to her teacher next week."

"Good. I had one recently, so she knows the situation now,

but I'd like you to talk to her, because you understand exactly how Caroline is doing."

"How did the reading of the will go? Was your mother there?"

"She was there and regrets she won't be here to see Caroline."

"Oh, Will. I'm glad we didn't tell Caroline her grandmother was in town. She doesn't need the slightest rejection."

"Ava, I have a half sister," he said. She turned with a wide-eyed gaze while he briefly told her about the bombshell. As he spoke, all he could think was that he'd missed Ava and wanted to be alone with her now. And that he was grateful to have her here to share this news with him.

"You'll have to meet your half sister."

He turned to face her. "I miss you, Ava."

"Will, let it go," she said, shaking her head.

"Go out with me this Saturday. Just a night out."

"Thank you, but no."

"You're going back to Austin when your job here is over?"

"No, I'm not," she said and his hope flared. "I hired an agency to look for land here. Will, I can't just leave Caroline like that. If I stay here in town I can still see her. If that's okay."

"Of course, it's okay. So you're moving here," he said, relief filling him.

"Yes, I am. She's precious, and to tell the truth, I'll miss her terribly and worry about her."

"She'll want you to stay, I'm sure."

"I've already told her. I'll come by on weekdays after school. I should be gone by the time you get home."

"You don't have to be gone by the time I get home. I want to see you," he said, taking her hand.

"Uncle Will!" Caroline's high-pitched voice carried.

Will rose to saunter to the pool to talk to Caroline and a few minutes later, his brothers arrived.

Will spent some time with his brothers and Garrett, and when the men joined Caroline in the pool, Will finally had Ava to himself again.

"You have a half sister you've never known about," Ava mused.

"Yes. We still don't know anything about her. She didn't attend, even though she was notified about the reading. We don't know who she is or where she lives. All we have is a name."

"Will, you have to find out."

"Damn straight. She's inherited a bundle from Dad. Grady said she doesn't want it, but no one turns down the kind of money we're talking about. I'll contact her and see what we can learn," he said, his mind already off his half sister.

Ava looked enticing and he wanted her alone. He ached to make love to her. He could look at her all evening and he wished she would stay tonight in her suite. His life was beginning to feel empty when Ava wasn't around. He wanted her to hold, to love and to talk to. His home had never felt big or lonely or empty before, but now there were moments when it did. Those moments vanished when she arrived.

But time alone with her would have to wait—especially because his brothers and Garrett were climbing out of the pool, wanting to hear Caroline read them a story.

Before dinner, when the uncles and Garrett crowded round, Caroline sat beside Ava and read aloud. Still thrilled and grateful, Will watched Caroline for a few minutes until his attention switched to Ava. She was capable, smart, beautiful, sexy enough to take his breath away just thinking about kissing her. He wanted her desperately, yet she had made it clear she would not have an affair.

Desire scalded, keeping him on edge. He found it difficult to concentrate, to think of anything except her.

When Caroline finished the book, Zach, Ryan and Garrett

applauded and heaped praise on the smiling girl. In minutes she was in her uncle Ryan's lap while he read to her.

Zach walked over to Will on the far side of the room. "I see what you mean about the change in Caroline. I couldn't believe it until I saw her. I just told Ava again how fantastic this has been. And the little pooch is cute."

"Part of it is the dog which broke the silence, but I think a big part of it is Ava, who bonded with her. She hangs on Ava if you notice, which surprises me since she's never had a mother around."

"She just likes Ava. By the way, I think you're going to have to rethink your views of marriage. You looked like a zombie today until you got home to her. I never thought I'd recommend marriage, but I don't think you can handle having her walk out of your life."

"Sure I can," he said, the words sounding hollow and false in his own ears. "I've never had a problem with women leaving before. And Ava has an agenda that nothing will take her away from."

Zach sipped his cold beer. "Better find someone else quickly then and get her out of mind. If you're not going to marry her, you have to let her go."

"You're a real help," Will snapped.

After dinner Ava headed upstairs with Rosalyn to take Caroline to bed. Caroline held Ava's hand. Her books were tucked beneath her other arm, and Muffy trailed along behind them. Ava glanced back to see Will watching her. Her heartbeat skipped and her back tingled.

In Caroline's room, Muffy crawled into her crate and curled up, and Caroline changed into soft pink pajamas.

"I'll read her a story," Ava told Rosalyn, who nodded.

"Just call me when you're leaving and I'll come. I'll be in the front room," Rosalyn said.

Ava sat in the rocker and Caroline brought a book to her,

then climbed up into Ava's lap, leaning against her while Ava read. Caroline played with a lock of Ava's hair, reaching up to twist it around her fingers. Ava read softly, rocking and holding Caroline close. Her heart squeezed because she loved the little girl. It was almost time for school to start, and Ava's time would be up. She wouldn't see Caroline as much, but she didn't want to give up seeing her. She had fallen in love with Will, but she also loved Caroline and that love would last forever.

When Ava finished the book, she closed it. "I'll read one more. Do you want to get in bed and I'll lie down with you? Or do you want to stay here and rock?"

"In bed," Caroline whispered sleepily.

In minutes Caroline slipped beneath the blanket while Ava stretched out on top and opened the book to read. She placed one arm around Caroline, who snuggled close against her. "I love you, Miss Ava."

"I love you, too, Caroline," Ava said, meaning it with all her heart. "You're so precious," she added and kissed Caroline lightly on the temple. Caroline held the small brown bear close and looked at the book while Ava began to read.

Soon Caroline's breath was even and deep. Ava looked at her and saw she was asleep. She began to carefully extricate herself, cautiously removing her arm from beneath Caroline. She closed the book and sat up, standing.

Will stood in the doorway leaning against the doorjamb.

She drew a deep breath. "You surprised me," she whispered.

He entered the room, crossing to look down at Caroline. He kissed her cheek lightly and draped an arm across Ava's shoulders. "You're so good with her. My brothers and Garrett are thrilled."

"Three more bachelors. What do they know about kids and Caroline?" she said with a smile.

"They've all seen her locked in that silent world of grief. They're singing your praises, which are well deserved."

"I'm so glad for her. She'll be fine in school."

"I'm glad you'll still see her when school starts."

"I love her, Will," she said, looking away, then headed out of the room to where Rosalyn sat.

"She's asleep," Will said. "We'll leave her in your charge now."

Rosalyn smiled. "She's so happy. Ava, you've done the impossible."

"Thanks, Rosalyn. I still think Muffy has to get credit."

As they walked down the hall, Ava said, "I'll tell your brothers goodbye. I should leave now."

"You can stay awhile and enjoy my brothers and Garrett. They're all fun." Will reached the open door of her old suite. He stepped inside, pulling her in with him.

"Will anyone stay in here? If you need me to move my things—"

"Don't be ridiculous. They're staying in the other wing. My brothers know how to party, and they'll be up until wee hours, playing pool, swimming. You'll hear them. I'm not having them up here by Caroline. Or you, if you decide to stay here tonight."

Will wrapped his arms around her and pulled her close. "I want you here all the time, Ava," he whispered, kissing away any reply.

She held him tightly, knowing they had to go downstairs, and kissed him back freely, responding eagerly. Her heart pounded and she melted against his hard length. She wanted him with the desperate urgency she had felt before as if they hadn't made love.

"Ava," he said, framing her face with his hands. "Marry me."

Astonished, she looked into his dark eyes. Her heart pounded and she couldn't get her breath. She wanted to cry out "yes" and not think of anything else, but she knew better than to do that.

"You don't mean that, Will. You've never said you love me. You've told me over and over you want me. That's different."

"I want you. I've never wanted anyone more," he declared solemnly. "I can't do anything for thinking about you. I want you in my life all the time."

His words both were wonderful and hurt her. She was glad he wanted her, yet that's all it was, pure physical desire. Not a deep and lasting love. She had known real love once and she couldn't settle for less again.

"Do you want me because you see that as the only way to get me in your bed on a long-term basis? Do you want to marry me because it would be convenient for Caroline? I know it would please her. She makes that obvious, but we can't marry to please a child. Not even Caroline."

"Ava, I'm proposing to you," he said.

"I love you," she said, gazing into his brown eyes. "I've loved you most of this summer, but it's futile. I won't marry without love. Will, your heart isn't in your proposal."

"Of course, it is," he said. "Ava, I wouldn't propose lightly."

"I doubt if you've even thought about proposing for a long time. This is sudden because you desire me intensely. That's wonderful, Will, but I want more. I want it all. I want your heart and your commitment. In good times and in bad."

"Ava, you have all that. I've proposed to you—something I never expected to do, but you're special."

"'Never expected' I think covers it. You haven't given this a lot of thought and it hasn't come out of love. It's from desire and wanting an affair. I can't do that, Will. I want the real thing," she said, feeling as if her insides were breaking and shattering, her heart splintering into a million broken pieces like shattered crystal. She hurt and hoped he never realized how badly. Her hands were knotted and she felt as cold as ice even though it was a late summer evening.

He stared at her and she could see she had touched on an aspect that he didn't want to deal with. With her heartbeat still racing and longing pulling at her, she shook her head. "It won't work out for us, Will. I'm sorry, but it's impossible. I don't think you've thought your proposal through."

She waited while a clock ticked away the seconds.

"What I feel is love," he finally answered.

"What you feel is lust." She hurt all over and tears stung her eyes. She wanted to toss aside logic and accept his proposal, but she knew a spur of the moment proposal of marriage would lead to trouble. There hadn't been declarations of love. Will wanted an affair so badly he was reaching for a quick solution.

She wiped away tears swiftly and refused to let herself consider his proposal. Reality painted a clear picture that left only one answer—no. They could not marry and expect happiness. His family pattern would continue with another doomed marriage unless he could love her.

"I think I should go. The deep, lasting love doesn't exist for you. Without that, there's just no future for us, Will." She left in a rush, wanting to get away before she shed the tears that she held back.

She left the mansion, slipping out without telling his brothers goodbye, feeling she couldn't be around Will another minute without crying.

In her silent condo, she sobbed, falling across her bed to let go.

Three weeks later, school started for Caroline. Ava saw her the next day, waiting at the house when Caroline returned in the limo with Rosalyn.

The minute Caroline saw Ava she tossed down her books

to dash to hug Ava, Muffy excitedly rushing around the girl's legs.

"Tell me about school," Ava said, listening while Caroline talked, marveling how much she had changed since Ava first met her.

Ava heard about school and was thrilled that Caroline was happy, smiling, talking about her new friend, Kellie. Ava spent an hour, then kissed Caroline goodbye and drove home while she could still avoid seeing Will. That night she called him to ask if Caroline could stay with her Saturday afternoon and overnight. After they made arrangements, they talked another three hours. When she hung up, she looked at the phone. "You're not out of my life yet, Will Delaney. You should be, but you're not." She missed him more instead of less. He had been friendly, flirted with her, but hadn't asked her out again. Had he given up? She loved him and his proposal haunted her. She missed him more each day and the moments she saw him at his mansion were the best time of day.

Saturday morning she was eager to see Caroline. She dressed in cutoffs and a red knit shirt, ready for a day of play. She had been told Rosalyn would accompany Caroline in the limo and that tomorrow Will would pick her up. She was glad she wouldn't see Will today; she needed to keep her focus on Caroline—not her shattered heart.

At three, when the limo pulled up, Ava ran to get Caroline's presents—books and a little coat for the brown bear, plus a pink bandanna for Muffy—returning just as the bell rang. Smiling with joy at the prospect of seeing Caroline, she flung open the door. "Come—" She stopped, looking up at Will.

Twelve

"Where's Caroline? Is she all right?" she asked, going cold while her heart raced.

Will stepped inside and closed the door, taking the present from her to set it on a table.

"Caroline's fine and you'll see her very soon. I wanted to talk to you first."

"She's waiting in the car?"

"No, she's home. I let her know she'll be seeing you very soon."

"Will, what on earth?" she asked, calming down, but becoming annoyed, yet aware of how handsome he looked in jeans and a charcoal knit shirt. "You scared me to pieces. I thought something happened to her."

He pulled her into his arms. "I came over to do this right. I've been thinking about us."

"There just is no 'us,'" she said, her exasperation fading as she saw the desire in his dark eyes. "You don't get that," she added, her voice changing, becoming breathless while her pulse speeded.

"Ava, I went about this all wrong. I told you I want you in my life. I've thought for hours about what you said. I want you to marry me," he said, withdrawing a black box from his pocket and holding it out to her.

She stared at it, but wouldn't touch it. "Will, we've been over this and why it won't work."

"It will work. I love you. I'm sorry I couldn't tell you so the other night. I didn't even know what love really is, until I met you."

Startled, she drew a deep breath and her heart began to pound faster.

"Ava, I'll support you in whatever you do. I want to marry you."

"What about your father's marriage and your brother's marriage?"

"You're not like my mother or like Lauren. I can have a happy marriage if it's with you. I love you with all my heart. I need you in too many ways to count. I want to share my life with you. Will you marry me?" he asked again, holding the box higher.

"Are you sure? You mean it? You've really thought this through?"

"I have. I've never been happier than this summer when you lived with us, when we made love and when you're there for Caroline. I want you back, love. Really want you."

"Will, you've been so bitter about marriage. This is a complete turnaround."

"Love does things to people. I just know you're part of my life now and I have to keep it that way. I need you, Ava. I love you, want you, need you. You're necessary to me." He knelt on one knee and took her hand. "Ava, will you marry me?"

"Will," she said, exhaling, her heart pounding while joy surged.

"Ava, please marry me," he repeated, standing again.

"You're sure?"

"Absolutely. Marriage. Forever commitment. That's what I want from you."

With a scream of delight, she threw her arms around him and hugged him. She kissed him, startling him for only a second and his arms banded her waist tightly and he leaned over her to kiss her passionately.

She tore her mouth away. "Yes, Will, I'll marry you," she cried and returned to kissing him. He picked her up, pausing a moment.

"Where's the bedroom?"

She pointed and they kissed again.

Later, she lay in his arms. "Will, I don't have the box you gave me." She started to roll off the bed, but he caught her and pulled her back.

"I'll get it," he said. He left and she watched him, relishing the sight of his virile body and long legs. He climbed back in bed to hold the velvet box and open it.

She gasped at the huge glittering diamond set in a gold band with diamonds on either side. "Will, that is shamefully large."

"No, it isn't. I want you to have it. I love you, Ava."

He slipped the ring on her finger. "Let's have the wedding soon."

"Very soon," she whispered. She studied the beautiful ring. "I can't wait to call my sisters and tell them. They'll have to be in my bridal party."

"Fine. I'll have my brothers and Garrett and another close friend, Tyler."

"Will, what about this half sister your family has discovered? Perhaps you can invite her?"

"She didn't even have an interest in inheriting a fortune. She won't be interested in meeting us or coming to a wedding. My brothers and I are still trying to contact her, but I'm not trying again until after the wedding and our honeymoon.

I don't have time for such a big distraction right now. Also, before I announce the news of our impending nuptials to my brothers, I want to tell Caroline."

Ava smiled. "She'll be so happy."

He nodded. "I sat her down this morning and told her I was going to ask you to marry me and if I could come see you instead of her. I told her whatever you said, I would come back and get her."

"Oh, my goodness. She may be anxious and waiting. Let's go tell her," Ava said, stepping out of bed. "I'll shower and we'll go." She gathered her clothes and looked at him. He lay with his hands behind his head, a smile on his face as he watched her. She yanked clothes in front of herself. "Will, get up. Let's shower and tell Caroline."

"I won't miss this."

She tried to cover herself, smiling all the way down the hall.

"Will, I can't stop looking at this ring," Ava said on the ride over to the mansion.

"Look all you want while I look at you," he said, pulling her close against his side.

They found Caroline in her playroom with Muffy and Rosalyn. Will had already called Rosalyn to tell her the news and that they wanted to share it with Caroline. The moment they arrived, Rosalyn greeted them with a big smile and headed upstairs.

Caroline's eyes were questioning and she looked intently at Will. He picked her up and put his other arm around Ava, pulling her close.

"Caroline, I told you I wanted to ask Ava to marry me, which I did. She accepted."

Caroline grinned broadly, looking at Ava. "Will you live here again?"

"Yes, I will live here again," Ava said, putting an arm

around Caroline so they formed a circle. "You will be my little girl."

"Caroline, your daddy will always be your daddy, but if you want to just call me Will, that might be easier for you. And if you want, I'm sure it would be all right with Ava if you call her Mommy."

Caroline looked at Ava who nodded as she smiled again. She glanced back at Will. "I'll call you Daddy Two."

They all laughed while they hugged. Ava had tears of joy that spilled over her cheeks. "Will, Caroline, this is the happiest day of my life."

"Let's pick a wedding date. Caroline, you can be our flower girl."

The little girl beamed.

Epilogue

Ava stood in the narthex of the church, holding Caroline's hand. Her sisters and close friends waited until the signal and then they began the walk down the aisle. The friends went first, next Summer and finally Trinity, who was maid of honor.

After Trinity, Ava bent to kiss Caroline. In her silk-and-tulle dress, the same shade of blue as the bridesmaids', Caroline looked like a doll. She smiled at Ava and started down the aisle with a basket of rose petals on her arm.

Ava's heart beat with joy while she watched Caroline carefully scatter rose petals as she walked down the aisle.

When Ava kissed her father's cheek, he patted her arm. "I hope you live long and happily," he whispered and she smiled in return.

Trumpets sounded and the wedding march began. Rising to their feet, guests turned while the wedding planner motioned to Ava to start down the aisle.

The groomsmen in their black tuxedos were handsome, all

tall and each one smiling. When her gaze flew to Will, her heart skipped with joy. Her handsome husband-to-be stood smiling at her, his gaze locked with hers. They would bind their lives together forever and Caroline now would be her little girl, too.

Joy reigned supreme as Ava could not stop smiling. She paused to give her mother a rose. Will's mother had been unable to attend, something he accepted without surprise. Ava gave another rose to Rosalyn, who sat alone on the opposite side of the aisle.

Finally, Ava's father placed her hand in Will's and she went through her vows in a daze of happiness.

Afterward at the country club reception, she danced with Will. "This is the happiest day of my life."

"Mine, too. We have a week to ourselves and then we'll come back to get Caroline and take her to Florida where she can meet all the princesses she wants."

"Will, this is paradise. I am so happy."

"Not half as happy as I am. You've given us so much joy and I am so in love with you, I shock myself. Caroline is radiant with our marriage. She loves you and loves having a mother."

"I know. I love her."

"Do we really have to stay for this reception?"

She laughed. "Of course, we have to. Everyone is here to see and talk to us."

"No, they're not. They're here to eat and dance and have a good time with friends. My brothers and Garrett are here for the reasons I just named."

"Maybe your family, but otherwise, they are here to see us, so we stay."

"I'll try, but I can't wait to get you alone. I want to peel you out of that dress and kiss you from head to toe."

"Will, you stop that now. Smile and dance and behave."

"Impossible." He grinned and spun her around.

"Will, I want Caroline to have a little brother or sister."

"We will get started on that soon. Very soon," he said, his arm tightening around her waist.

She laughed, thinking she was the luckiest woman on earth to have such a handsome, wonderful husband and an adorable little girl.

* * * * *

PASSION

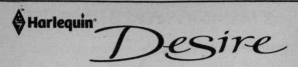

Harlequin® Desire

COMING NEXT MONTH
AVAILABLE JUNE 12, 2012

#2161 HIS MARRIAGE TO REMEMBER
The Good, the Bad and the Texan
Kathie DeNosky

#2162 A VERY PRIVATE MERGER
Dynasties: The Kincaids
Day Leclaire

#2163 THE PATERNITY PROMISE
Billionaires and Babies
Merline Lovelace

#2164 IMPOSSIBLE TO RESIST
The Men of Wolff Mountain
Janice Maynard

#2165 THE SHEIKH'S REDEMPTION
Desert Knights
Olivia Gates

#2166 A TANGLED AFFAIR
The Pearl House
Fiona Brand

REQUEST YOUR FREE BOOKS!
2 FREE NOVELS PLUS 2 FREE GIFTS!

ALWAYS POWERFUL, PASSIONATE AND PROVOCATIVE

YES! Please send me 2 FREE Harlequin Desire® novels and my 2 FREE gifts (gifts are worth about $10). After receiving them, if I don't wish to receive any more books, I can return the shipping statement marked "cancel." If I don't cancel, I will receive 6 brand-new novels every month and be billed just $4.30 per book in the U.S. or $4.99 per book in Canada. That's a saving of at least 14% off the cover price! It's quite a bargain! Shipping and handling is just 50¢ per book in the U.S. and 75¢ per book in Canada.* I understand that accepting the 2 free books and gifts places me under no obligation to buy anything. I can always return a shipment and cancel at any time. Even if I never buy another book, the two free books and gifts are mine to keep forever.

225/326 HDN FEF3

Name _____ (PLEASE PRINT) _____

Address _____ Apt. # _____

City _____ State/Prov. _____ Zip/Postal Code _____

Signature (if under 18, a parent or guardian must sign) _____

Mail to the **Reader Service:**
IN U.S.A.: P.O. Box 1867, Buffalo, NY 14240-1867
IN CANADA: P.O. Box 609, Fort Erie, Ontario L2A 5X3

Not valid for current subscribers to Harlequin Desire books.

Want to try two free books from another line?
Call 1-800-873-8635 or visit www.ReaderService.com.

* Terms and prices subject to change without notice. Prices do not include applicable taxes. Sales tax applicable in N.Y. Canadian residents will be charged applicable taxes. Offer not valid in Quebec. This offer is limited to one order per household. All orders subject to credit approval. Credit or debit balances in a customer's account(s) may be offset by any other outstanding balance owed by or to the customer. Please allow 4 to 6 weeks for delivery. Offer available while quantities last.

Your Privacy—The Reader Service is committed to protecting your privacy. Our Privacy Policy is available online at www.ReaderService.com or upon request from the Reader Service.

We make a portion of our mailing list available to reputable third parties that offer products we believe may interest you. If you prefer that we not exchange your name with third parties, or if you wish to clarify or modify your communication preferences, please visit us at www.ReaderService.com/consumerschoice or write to us at Reader Service Preference Service, P.O. Box 9062, Buffalo, NY 14269. Include your complete name and address.

HDES11B

red-hot reads

Fall under the spell of fan-favorite author

Leslie Kelly

Workaholic Mimi Burdette thinks she's satisfied dating the
handsome man her father has picked out for her. But when sexy
firefighter Xander McKinley moves into her apartment building,
Mimi finds herself becoming…distracted. When Mimi opens a
fortune cookie predicting who will be the man of her dreams,
then starts having erotic dreams, she never imagines Xander
is having the same dreams! Until they come together
and bring those dreams to life.

Blazing Midsummer Nights

The magic begins June 2012

Saddle up with Harlequin® series books this summer
and find a cowboy for every mood!

Available wherever books are sold.

USA TODAY *bestselling author Kathie DeNosky*
presents the first book in her brand-new miniseries,
THE GOOD, THE BAD AND THE TEXAN.

HIS MARRIAGE TO REMEMBER

Available June 2012 from Harlequin® Desire!

Brianna wasn't sure Sam would want her here. After all,
they were just one signature away from a divorce. But until
the dissolution of their marriage was final, they were still
legally married, which meant she was needed here.

As she turned to go through the hospital's Intensive Care
Unit doors to Sam's room, Brianna bit her lower lip to keep
it from trembling. Even though she and Sam were ending
their relationship, the very last thing she wanted was to see
him harmed.

"Does your head hurt, Sam?" she asked.

He reached for her hand. "Don't worry, sweetheart. I'm
going to be just fine. If you'll get my clothes, I'll get dressed
and we can go home. Hell, I'll even let you play nurse."

Why was Sam insisting they go home together? She
had moved out of the ranch house three months ago. His
obvious lack of memory bothered her. She needed to speak
to the doctor about it right away. "Try to get some rest.
We'll deal with everything in the morning."

Sam didn't look happy, but he finally nodded. Then he
pinned her with his piercing blue gaze. "Are you doing all
right?"

Confused, she nodded. "I'm doing okay. Why do you
ask?"

"You told me you were going to get one of those preg-
nancy tests at the drug store," Sam said, giving her hand a

gentle squeeze. "Were we successful? Are you pregnant?"

A cold, sinking feeling settled in the pit of her stomach. He didn't remember. She had miscarried in her seventh week, and that had been almost six months ago. Something was definitely wrong.

"No, I'm not pregnant," she said. "Now, get some rest. I'll be in later to check on you."

"It's going to be hard to do without you beside me," he said, giving her a grin.

Some things never changed, she thought as she left to find the neurologist. The sun rose in the east. The ocean rushed to shore. And Sam Rafferty could make her knees weak with nothing more than his sexy-as-sin smile.

What will Brianna do if Sam never remembers the truth?

Find out in Kathie DeNosky's new novel
HIS MARRIAGE TO REMEMBER

Available June 2012 from Harlequin® Desire!